The Week

The Week

Joanna Ruocco

THE ELEPHANTS

The Elephants Ltd.

www.theelephants.net

ISBN 978-0-9953483-0-1 print

•••

Edited by Broc Rossell

Cover design by Drew Swenhaugen

CONTENTS

MANUFACTURED OBSOLESCENCE   1

TWILIGHT   5

PAPARAZZI   9

TINDER   11

RPG   14

HEDGE FUND   15

MAGNETIC NORTH   17

SOCIAL NETWORK   20

WEATHER.COM   21

DOWNTURN   27

TSUNAMI   29

BAD INFINITY   32

MANUFACTURED OBSOLESCENCE   33

FRIENDLY FIRE   36

WELL   41

EXCULPATORY CLAUSE   44

TALKING POINT   45

DEFENSE OF MARRIAGE ACT   49

THIRD-PARTY   51

MANUFACTURED OBSOLESCENCE   57

TERMINATOR   59

LEFT BEHIND   67

NEIGHBORHOOD WATCH   71

BACK TO THE FUTURE   73

PUBLIC EDUCATION   74

AGE OF MAJORITY   76

PUBLIC POLLING   79

RELIGIOUS CONFLICT   83

POCKET DIAL   86

OCCUPY   88

BAILOUT   90

PYRAMID SCHEMES   93

VOYAGER   98

THE BEST OF BEES   99

HUMANITIES   101

AGE DEFYING COVERAGE   104

PERMAFROST   106

BABY BOOMERS   107

FOXHOLES   112

SUPERDOME   116

TRANSITION TOWN   117

TRANSITION TOWN   119

PERFECT COMPETITION   123

MEME   124

CREUTZFELDT–JAKOB   127

TRANSITION TOWN   129

MANUFACTURED OBSOLESCENCE

I am tired of reading stories where a single thought, a woman's thought, generates a whole system of thoughts. The woman thinks her thought through and the story is just this thinking through of the thought. Sometimes there is a little framing material external to the thought. The woman is sitting at her desk, her desk at home. She is the kind of woman who sits at a desk at home, a woman without a regular job, an unobligated woman, a woman like me, only I sit at the kitchen table. I like to eat snacks when I am sitting. It bothers me to have food where it does not belong, on my desk; however, it does not bother me to have a computer on the kitchen table, or papers, or pens, or a stapler, or scissors, so I sit with these things and also food at the kitchen table. It bothers me to have coins on a kitchen table, and coins on a desk do not bother me, but I can sit without coins nearby.

The woman sitting at the desk is writing, or filing bills, or reading the small booklet she found attached to the cap of her moisturizer, and then she begins to think, or else she is sitting thinking, doing nothing, and either way, the material world external to the thought slowly becomes part of the thought, and the woman, thinking, becomes part of the thought, and so do the skin bumps the moisturizer would otherwise relieve with extra-rich emollients. The skin bumps are part of a system of thought, and the woman no longer needs the moisturizer. The skin bumps are at the same level of thought as the skin and, therefore, the skin is smooth. Of course only the woman, thinking at her desk, finds this to be true. As soon as she leaves her house, her skin is not smooth. She has bumps, her hair has thinned, her teeth are stained, her figure is not tidy, the clothing she wears emphasizes her displeasing proportions, she smells like her cat and like the scalded milk she feeds to her cat, a musty, souring smell, and this is how she appears to others: awkward, rumpled, stinky. She can't appear to herself; that's not how eyes work. She can only appear to others. This is good for the woman: to appear to others and not herself. It works like this:

Say the woman sees another woman exiting a bungalow across the street. The bungalow is even less lofty, less imposing than the average bungalow. It's a below-average bungalow in every way. One story, no porch, no dormers. The woman is pretty sure it's off plumb. It is a crooked shack on a patchy dog-pitted quarter lot, but there are no shacks in the woman's neighborhood, so, no, it is a below-average bungalow. The woman exiting the bungalow is hard-working and well-groomed. She doesn't sit at a desk in her bedroom. She has bills to pay and a body to maintain. Her hair is dark. Her scalp is clean. She takes care of business, this woman. No one has given her any breaks in life but she is smart, ambitious, attractive, and willing to put in extra hours. She makes her own luck. There she goes, exiting the bungalow, walking fast, no time to waste, even though her footwear is impractical, worse than impractical—constrictive, steeply pitched highly unstable platforms limiting blood flow to the toes and stressing the muscles of the lower back, the sort of footwear that might be confused with an implement of torture if described by an anthropologist unfamiliar with the culture—and she's eating a handful of almonds as she walks. This woman can't appear to herself any more than the first woman can appear to herself. She strides down the sidewalk and she appears to the other woman, the horse-faced, cat-smelling woman who has exited her adorable Victorian and who now appears to her. Each is the appearance of woman for the other.

The woman whose thought generates this story does not have to worry about taking care of her own body. She does not have to worry about grooming, dieting, exercising, dressing, because she understands that the other woman is the form of her appearance in the world. She has gotten the better end of the deal. Her system of thought has subsumed the world, and in that world the other woman presents the toned body that gives her flabby body form. It isn't fair. The woman whose thought generates this story doesn't do any work. That's the class bias of philosophy.

In this kind of story, that's a conclusion. That's the end of the story. It's over. I'm tired. Okay.

TWILIGHT

What is the quickest way to become a good person? This is an important question. There are many causes competing for our time and money and most of the causes are not administered efficiently; a large fraction of your time and money goes not to the cause but to other things, things that do not make you a good person, like web maintenance. A pit latrine might make you a good person, but how much time and money would you have to give to a cause before it equaled one pit latrine? You could go somewhere and build a pit latrine yourself, with your own two hands, in the dust, in the sun, but first you should remember that you do not shit in pit latrines. You have a flush-toilet. Even if you've never thought about liking the flush-toilet you will probably admit it's better than a pit latrine. Why are you building a pit latrine instead of bathrooms with flush-toilets? This is the problem with causes. They are wrong-headed. You will misstep. You will not have done the right thing. Are you a good person if you do bad things? All of this thinking is not quick. Listen, this is quick. Go and donate one pint of blood. This will take an hour. Go and donate another pint of blood. Go and donate another pint of blood. Do it twelve times. Even traveling from blood drive to blood drive you can get it all done in one day. Maybe you're a small person and you only have ten pints of blood to give. That's okay! Every person can only give as much blood as he or she has, six pints, eight pints, ten pints, twelve pints of blood. If your iron is low, that's okay, you can give anyway, and if you have tattoos or sex partners or you have spent time in sub-Saharan Africa, or if you are sub-Saharan African, or if you have a blood borne pathogen or weigh ninety pounds or just turned eleven or were alive in the seventies, it's okay, no one will say anything, the needle goes in and the blood goes out along the tube into pint sack after pint sack after pint sack, no questions asked, and soon all of the blood will be out of your body, and if you give as much blood as you have, and you bring a friend, and your friend gives as much blood as she has, and your friend brings a friend, or two friends, and those friends bring friends, before very long all of the people will have given all of their blood, all of the blood will be outside all of the people, all of the blood non-violently removed from all of the people everywhere on the planet. Listen, because this is how to be good, this giving of blood, this giving of pint after pint of your blood; this is the best, quickest, most wonderful thing you can do. It is better than founding an international orphanage for peace. It is better than sheltering rescue dogs or transforming vacant lots into gardens or getting appointed UN-ambassador or researching anti-cancer vaccines. It is better than moving into the forest, living off the grid alone in the forest, even if you wash beneath a cold-water pump, even if you only eat ferns, even if you plant six trees for every one you cut down. Listen right at this minute, there are eighty billion pints of blood inside people on the planet. That's ten billion gallons! There are ten million in-ground swimming pools in the United States of America. On average, one in-ground swimming pool contains twenty-two thousand gallons of water. Every pint of blood inside every person on the planet could still not fill all the swimming pools in the United States of America, but that's okay! Enough swimming pools could be filled with blood to make a stunning visual impression, from up close, but from the air especially. You would see the suburbs inset with jewel-bright kidney beans, and darker beans too, and ovals and squares; the suburbs would tessellate darkly and ripple with shining black layers of flies, and every pint of blood from inside every person on the planet would dry at last into fragrant dust, garnet dust, and every pint of blood from inside every person on the planet

would lift into the wind and snow down like shatter-
ing a nitrogen rose. We would all be a part of it. We
would all be together a part of it, all of us, the explo-
sion of the same human rose. The beautiful must not
be confused with the good—I read that somewhere,
something like it, carved in a rock. But listen, don't
you want, deep down, to be a beautiful person? Isn't
that the thing you really want? Don't you want to
become good just so that you can finally be beautiful?
Well now you know how. The only trick is to keep your
heart beating, to keep your heart pushing the blood
through the tube, not to give up the whole while, to
push and to push, until the valve sucks air.

PAPARAZZI

It is best to be a mediocre person, a person that can be easily replaced. In the succession of generations, there will be many people who think and do what you think and do, and who inspire the same kinds of feelings in other people that you yourself inspire in other people, and you know that it works the other way too, that before you were born there were people who thought and did what you think and do, with adjustments made for available technologies and prevailing opinions, and you are the replacement for at least one of these people, and it would be comforting for the loved ones of the person you replaced if these loved ones traveled through time and encountered you. Even without traveling through time, this sort of thing happens. You meet a person and the person reminds you of another person; the person is the same kind of person as the other person, and you can make space in your brain by realizing that many people are actually one person with different names and faces and not always in the same city; one person is in many places and as soon as you meet them you know plenty about them, even though it is hard remember which name to call them by. Some men always call their girlfriends by the same name. This can mean a man calls his girlfriends Rachel, Rachel, Rachel, although often, because he is a linear thinker and believes that sequence must be a form of progression, he adds numerals, Rachel 1, Rachel 2, Rachel 3, or it can mean he calls his girlfriends, babe, babe, babe; the point is that it doesn't matter what he calls them; many girls are actually one girlfriend. There is no reason to be angry when this happens, when you are called Rachel, when you are called babe, when a time-traveler looks at you meltingly and reaches out for your hand. It is much worse to be a special person, an irreplaceable person, a person who dies one time and is lost to everything forever and who is lonely the whole time she is alive.

TINDER

I am in the park. I see a circle of mothers. The mothers are circuit training under the cottonwood trees and the circle of circuit-training mothers is circled by baby strollers and the baby strollers are circled by squirrels and the squirrels keep coming, more and more squirrels dropping down from the trees, army-crawling head first down the trees, joining the thickening circle of squirrels, the circle that unbeknownst to the mothers had cordoned off the circle of strollers. The mothers do not notice the squirrels. The mothers maintain a singular focus on fitness. They stow their nuts and their bars with their babies in strollers. I see the circle of squirrels close in—close in on the strollers—and I see the first wave of squirrels swarm up the strollers, and the mothers running in place with high knees, the mothers squat-thrusting, tuck-jumping, the mothers revving, pumping their bodies, they have the glow of young mothers. I like their hair and their work-out clothes and the way they wave their tiny bright weights, and I think about stopping the squirrels before they can summit the strollers, before they can cover the babies, pile on the babies and eat the babies' whole faces, but then I think about thinking.

I stop and I think about thinking, how thinking intervenes between regular people and heroes. There's a split-second for heroes, and if you think about heroes or seconds or mothers or babies or how many squirrels, that's it for the faces; you're standing still in the park thinking through circles in circles, and things happen around you. The strollers seethe with squirrels. The mothers leg-lift in plank. The sun is hot but the air is cold and geese are passing through it. You've never seen so many geese flying one by one, the geese composed of a lone goose and then another lone goose, each lone goose flying close to the ground. There are many of them but they aren't in any way geese. Each goose chooses its own direction. Each goose stretches out its very long neck and chases its own head through the air. A goose goes by. Across the street from the park, there's South High School with a goose landing on the lawn. There's a goose much closer, by the adult athletic equipment. It's emerging from a bed of ornamental kale, lifting off, wings thrashing the crimpled edges of the kale. The squirrels have devoured the nuts and the bars, the babies, the strollers. The mothers are sweating. The leaves on the cottonwood trees are a rattling yellow. There are yellow leaves on the lake. There's a lone goose on the edge in long weeds. There's a squirrel in profile—one rolling eye. It is holding its paws to its mouth. Some squirrels can fly but no one ever sees them. Flying squirrels are shy. The shyness helps them survive. They fly short flights from their trees in the night. They don't mingle. They hide from predators and from each other and so they don't breed very often. They are dying out. Each one that's alive stays alive helped by shyness, but each one stays shyly alive all alone. The squirrels that fly are dying out slowly, without violence, in whole moments: no heroics. Things happen around them while they sleep, each in the crotch of a tree, resting up for the short flights they take at moon rise, short flights without encounters, short flights that keep their muscles from fraying so they can sleep day after day curled in the crotches of trees. I've never seen one. I walk around at night and I try not to encounter anything, although I can't help but observe small disturbances. My rule of thumb is to give disturbances distance. When I identify a center I move to a perimeter. Often I walk for a very long while. From time to time I remember to return to my daylight haunts. I collect the broken roughage from the public beds.

RPG

What makes mothers a horde is their will to cross
the river. They kindle fires. They pitch tents in motile
darkness. All night they cook or they use the pots to
birth in. At dawn they bury embers, replace the lids.
In the water, they breathe through reeds. They float
in the shadows beneath the bridges. They detonate
remotely, bursting under the pressure of their daughters' daughters' hands.

HEDGE FUND

One day she woke up having invented the best ever trail mix. She remembered the trail mix contained soft purple seaweed, dried golden mulberries, shiitake mushrooms thoroughly cooked but still woody, and one more thing that unified but diversified the other flavors. She thought it was a very dry thing, a powdery thing that absorbed the sliminess of the mushrooms. This dry thing must be present in a very small amount because too much of the dry thing would absorb all the mushroom slime and the mushroom slime served an important purpose in the trail mix. The mushroom slime softened the seaweed. That was the secret to the seaweed not cutting up your mouth. Maybe the dry thing was just a little bit of chopped up sweet hay or grasshoppers, but those things did not seem right, maybe it was grated sarsaparilla. For awhile, lying there, she felt disappointed that she couldn't be certain what the dry thing was, but then she felt

exhilarated to begin the process of discovery. The journey would take her far from her bed out the front door
and through the streets of the town. It would take her
into house after house, where she would investigate
thoroughly, on her hands and knees, licking the old
plaster that crumbled from cracks in the walls, sniff-
ing the garlic skins behind every breadbox.

MAGNETIC NORTH

You can adopt dogs and children. You can adopt bus
stops. You can't adopt the homeless. This is because
the homeless are too fragile. The homeless are a delicate ecosystem. You can't just de-worm the homeless, pick their nits and clean them, take them inside
and care for them. This sounds like a good thing to do,
at least as good as doing the same for a dog, a two-
pound mix from the Chihuahua rescue, but it is an
ignorant thing to do. It oversimplifies the issue with
the homeless. You can't take the homeless inside. The
homeless belong where they are, in the open. They
are part of the open. The open is very complex. It is
made of microbes and the water cycle, air and the ele-
ments and the homeless in proportions impossible to
reproduce in the home. If you take the homeless out
of the open, you change the open. You damage the
open and in so-doing you damage the homeless. The
homeless are too important to damage. If we didn't

have the homeless, we wouldn't have homes. If we didn't have homes, we wouldn't have the homeless. The homeless are not a feature of homes, but they are essential to every feature of homes, crouching downhill from the homes, facing the massy façades of the homes, the pilasters, pediments, brick work, friezes, bracketed eaves, the turret dormers, the two-story porte-cocheres; the homeless press against the bulwarks of homes. This vital tension constitutes homes. It is a harmony: the homeless and homes. They come into being together. It is a balance, not unbeautiful. A neither unbeautiful nor beautiful balance. When you adopt a bus stop you put a sign near the bus stop. You put a trash can near the bus stop. You put wrappers in the can. You rearrange a few things, but you don't change the balance; you don't tamper with the balance like you would if you adopted the homeless. The balance is actually quite tenuous. We need to be more careful. What if the world turned upside down? What if the iron center of the Earth switched charge and repelled the crust? When you walk down the hill from your home, you must walk briskly. You must keep to the path. You must notice only cultivated flowers. If you glimpse in the weeds, through the rain, the rain falling on the necks of the homeless as they nod in the way of the homeless, rain on their necks and in the palms of their upturned hands, you must rush by. You must not disturb the homeless. They are facing the

facades of homes and you must not interpose your face .
between their faces and the facades of the homes. You
must not look in their faces. Look away. Hurry back
home. Even the observer effect, well documented by
physicists and psychologists, could ruin what we all
have here.

SOCIAL NETWORK

When you have been eating for long enough, the food begins to resemble you. This means it also looks like people in your family. The very best food looks like everyone.

WEATHER.COM

The temperature that makes you comfortable naked is the perfect temperature and less perfect is the range of temperatures that require some kind of covering. You need to put on a layer or layers of something, cotton or denim or wool, or blended fabric or high-performance fully synthetic fabric engineered out of chemicals, and wearing that layer or layers enables you to experience the temperature as perfect, although of course it is not, it is not naturally perfect. In the past, when you saw people wrapped up in a layer or layers of something, you knew this. You knew the temperature wasn't perfect for people. In the Pleistocene, for example, you saw people walking single file each wrapped in the pelt of a giant ground sloth and you knew the temperature was perfect for ground sloths but that people, naked, would not be comfortable. Or you saw, on the edge of a great hot bog, a bog under the crusted surface of which a methane fire smoldered, people sitting in young ferns, entirely naked, and you knew the temperature was perfect for people. In other words, the sight of a person, naked or not naked, used to convey information about the perfection or imperfection of temperature. Nowadays, things are very different. Legal, ethical, and aesthetic systems are in place that regulate nakedness. Temperature is a factor but it's no longer the deciding factor. It's a factor, but only within socially established limits. If you saw outside your window, people totally naked, naked people standing at the bus stop, you wouldn't think "Wonderful—the temperature is perfect today" and plan accordingly, gathering your wallet, keys, and shopping list, putting on your flat shoes but leaving your cotton, denim, wool, blended, or synthetic layers untouched in the dresser drawers. You would think, "Those people are making some kind of a statement" and you would consider the possible meanings of their nakedness in context. Nowadays nakedness takes on meaning without reference to temperature. Nakedness has been disconnected from natural causes. It has been made arbitrary so it can signify within the legal, ethical, and aesthetic systems people have created.

Here's an example: nowadays, legally, in public, nakedness is prohibited. It's also unethical, and in most cases aesthetically unpleasing. Even if the temperature is perfect, you will not see naked people at the bus stop, unless, of course, those people are, in fact, making some kind of statement, a statement about surviving cancer perhaps, or stopping war or ageism or the overuse of antibiotics. You will almost always see people covered, at least partially, in a layer or layers, but this covering of their nakedness doesn't indicate, first and foremost, imperfection in the temperature but rather subjection to ideology, which is nice to know about but not useful if your main concern is temperature, how best to gauge and prepare for it in a given moment. Nowadays, because people are subjects of ideology, you can't assume, if you see the people at the bus stop in shirts and slacks or blouses and skirts, that they wouldn't be more comfortable naked, that is, you can't assume that the temperature isn't perfect. Nor can you assume, if you see, as you do rarely or never, naked people at the bus stop, that nakedness equals perfect temperature. Nowadays nakedness always equals something else.

Of course, it's different in private. In their private houses, people are free to be naked because different legal, ethical, and aesthetic standards apply in the private versus public domain. If you look through a person's window, that person's nakedness or layering of fabrics will let you gauge the perfection of the temperature, but only inside that person's house, where the temperature is also private and has nothing to do with the temperature outside the house, or for that matter, with the temperature inside any other house, however close by. Knowing how perfect the temperature is inside another person's house does not tell you how to prepare for anything but entering that person's house, and legal and ethical regulations are in place to prevent that.

Across the street from my house, there is a house and I have observed, through the window, a girl dancing in her bedroom in the house. She dances naked, which means that the temperature in her bedroom is, when she is at rest, slightly imperfect, but by moving around vigorously, she is able to agitate the particles that constitute matter until the temperature is perfect. "Motion of the particles that constitute matter" is a way of describing temperature, and the girl has found a way to move the matter in and around her body so as to establish perfection. I have never seen anyone so comfortable as the girl dancing, the matter in and around her body moving nearly as though it were all of a piece.

Once, the girl saw me through her window as I stood looking at her through my window--she ducked down and her light in the window went out. I turned out my light too and stood again at my window but my eyes did not adjust sufficiently to make her out through the darkness. Standing in my bedroom, I wear a cotton layer, but when I dance in my bedroom, agitating particles, I take the layer off. I

dance naked as comfortably as the girl, but a different dance from the girl's dance because the temperature in my bedroom was not the same to begin with.
Nowadays, in public you need to disconnect from
everything natural, you need to wrap yourself with a
layer or layers whether the temperature is perfect or
imperfect, but in private you can connect the matter
in your body with the matter around it. You can sit
or stand or move around naked until you are so comfortable it's like you don't exist. There's just particles
in a room.

Sometimes, though, in private, you can go too far.
You can dance too vigorously, dance so vigorously the
agitation of particles in and around your body is too
much, imperfect in a new way. The discomfort is acute.
Sometimes, alone in my bedroom, I do this. I dance
until I can't bear it, until my skin itself is an unbear-
able layer. I want in those moments to be even more
naked than naked. I want to remove the top layer of
my nakedness. I don't know how often this has been
done. It was done, perhaps, frequently in the past but
is done less frequently now, when skin has become a
synecdoche for subject and subjects are produced by
ideology and so removing a layer or layers of skin is
impossible, the part is always the whole. All I know
is that for certain long moments, in the night, in my
bedroom, I'm naked, I'm dancing, and then I can no
long bear it. Beneath the topmost layer, there is, if I

slice very finely, a layer, and beneath this layer a layer, and then there's something else, a new kind of layer. What is it? I don't know. It's not quite a layer. Behind her dark window, the girl can see it all happen. A person backlit in a bedroom, a naked person, and then part of a person, a partial person, which today is not a person. Not "is." Not "person." The girl won't think, "That's a person making a statement." In this case, there's no person. There's no statement. What I'm saying is there is no way to prepare.

DOWNTURN

The universe curved and there was a massive occurrence of gravity and people stopped floating off the planet and my brother bought a dump truck because he knew the future lay in weight and who could move it. The horse shit stayed on the ground now and the cow shit and the pellets of the leveret that used to look so sweet and small against the sky and my brother became a man of tonnage in our eyes, a man of potentially infinite tonnage, my brother driving up and down the road his brimful dump truck with its wreath of steam. He dumped and dumped, my enterprising brother, and soon there was a mountain in the yard, and we watched it grow and we ate a little bread and liver and we waved to my brother as he drove. He drove. He cranked the big wheel. When my brother's dumping ended we ringed our bodies around the mountain. It had mass and I climbed it, the good brown mountain. At the top I looked down—everything was there—and my heart sank through me like a plumb bob. I sank into the mountain and the mountain was warm and brown and squeezing and I got warmer inside of it. I was the warm core of the mountain, so deep in the mountain that I pulsed there undetected. My brother came nearer. He pulled his gloves off and they dropped and he trod them with his heavy boots. He reached out to the mountain. I felt his fingers wander the cooling surface of the dome.

TSUNAMI

Don't get hung up on what you're hearing, that the wars of the future will be fought over water. Everything is water. Earth is solidified water; air is sublimated water; fire is sublimated air, or doubly sublimated water; water is water. Don't take it from me. This comes straight from the Greeks. I am telling you what the Greeks told me, not the current day Greeks, the old Greeks, via scrolls. The wars of the future will be fought over everything. For example, my brother knows you can infuse oil with mushroom spores. My brother has infused a biodegradable oil with spore-mass from several varieties of mushroom and this is the oil he uses to lubricate his chainsaw. When my brother cuts down the enemy with his chainsaw, he colonizes the bodies with mushrooms. Mushrooms cover the field of battle and my brother harvests the mushrooms. He makes teas from the mushrooms. The teas fight cancer. My brother calls this the war against cancer. Don't get sucked in to the war against cancer, leave that war to my brother; you can make your own war.

For example, I look at you, I count you, all of you; I count a certain number of carcasses. The Greeks called this "time." You can make a war against time. Obviously, these are fluid definitions — I'm not trying to say that war and the future aren't the same thing. You have the power to insert infinite combat between "before" and "after."

Start now. Don't trust your senses, which tell you that a person is mucus and plaque. Squeeze everyone; there's water, with a salt taste. What does that tell you? Don't believe what you've been hearing about survival. Think how you feel when you are eating. Think how you feel when you are being eaten. Eating is objective, but there is a subjective component. Do you understand what I'm saying? I'm not saying don't bury tins of sardines packed in oil alongside guns packed in oil; you should by all means bury the sardines and the guns. Government is breeding its secret army of humanzees. They call this the war on the self. You can be modified to glow or contain your own supply of nicotine or withstand the cold or open cans with your thumbs.

They can't yet undo all the damage of being born. They can web your toes, they can cut gills in the sides of your neck, they can reinforce your skin with asbestos fibers. I can take volunteers. I can take prisoners. First, kill your dependents. Not even war can be considered a means of direct communication.

BAD INFINITY

One thing is magic. One cup is magic. One mountain. One horn. One scepter. One sword. One of many brothers. Small clearing. Small house, wattle and tree moss. Several times upon a time is not the way to start a magic story. One day. One night. You are alone in the rotunda, pouring milk into a hat. There is one ivy. One myrtle. There is one star in the sky. There is one vapor between us. One back, the world's ballast. One neck outstretched for the black-hafted axe. The forest you ride through is girls in brown cotton. Shaken, one drops an apple. Another a daughter. Another swings open on a metal hinge.

MANUFACTURED OBSOLESCENCE

The story begins with a stable situation: a woman sitting at a desk. The woman is thinking. Something should perturb the situation, something outside of the woman's thought. The situation should become unstable. Then a counter-force should restore stability, but a different stability. Nothing is quite the same as it was before. This must happen. It must happen now. The woman is sitting thinking, at her desk, and a bat flies into the windowpane. It is daytime. Bats are rare in the neighborhood because bats prefer to live in caves, pines, eaves, and there are no caves or pines in the neighborhood, and there are below-average eaves in the neighborhood due to the preponderance of bungalows. Because of its eaves, with their shadowy lacework of gingerbread trim, the woman's adorable Victorian is the likeliest place to find bats in the neighborhood, but the woman can't remember the last time she saw bats careening around in the dusk.

Dusk is the woman's least favorite time to be out. People are coming home from work, or, in the summertime, people are walking around in their off hours. People abound at dusk and spoil it. Dusk should not be witnessed. It's the moment on the earth when a quantitative change becomes a qualitative change—when day becomes night—and it's delicate enough that the witnesses spoil it, spoil the moment. That's why the woman stays inside now at dusk. It's not *dusk* anymore. It's not the dusk from the woman's childhood, which would begin when she noticed the large white rock by the fencepost becoming luminous, because the old wood of the fencepost had dimmed, and the grass, and then she would see that all the objects in the yard were slowly rearranging themselves, not their positions but their potencies. The light energy of day, before it changed into the dark energy of night, created a pattern of fading and glowing things, and that pattern was dusk, but not anymore, not with all the people in the way. The woman hated them. She had known how to keep very still by the rock, by the fencepost, because a person must not walk in the dusk, a person must sit by a fence or by a gravestone or by a barrel or a ladder or the corner of a house, and she had known when dusk became more than itself, when more dusk became night. As a girl, the woman had kept so silent and still. She had let it all happen. She had been rearranged. She had been rearranged into girl and rock and fencepost and bats. That was dusk. She had made it. She was part of it. That's how it had happened. But the woman is no longer a girl. The woman is a woman and the girl is gone. Without the girl, the pattern is different, the dusk is different, spoiled. The woman has spoiled it. The girl is gone; the bats are gone; the woman has spoiled everything. The woman is the one. She has done it. That's why she stays inside. She doesn't join the people walking, the people looking for what the dusk was. It isn't safe. There's no pattern. There's no order of things. Now the day needs only the mildest pressure—the pressure of the people looking—to trigger the night. The shot can burst the windowpane at noon, it can make a hole in her chest and the darkness comes in.

FRIENDLY FIRE

Humans have drives. There is the sex drive. There is a drive for food, the food drive. The food drive might have a more basic name, the eat drive. "Eat" doesn't sound more basic than "food." They have the same kind of strong, basic sound, but eat is more basic than food. There are all kinds of foods but only one way to eat. You have to put the food in your mouth. You have to put some solid nutrimental thing inside your mouth and do something with your mouth, even if you don't masticate, even if all you do is push the thing down whole with the muscles of your tongue and throat.

They took out part of her friend's colon and stomach, and her uterus, but for awhile food still got into her stomach from her mouth, and traveled through her intestines and came out in the regular way; the food didn't taste like anything, but she put it in her mouth; she ate the food. It was eating. It's strange when food doesn't taste like anything. It's still eating, but you feel strange. You put the food in your mouth and it's good normal food but there's something wrong with your mouth. Your mouth doesn't make any saliva or the saliva drips out through your lips before you can stop it. Your cheek is between your molars when you move your molars on the food. Her friend didn't like this eating, but she did it. What else could she do? Humans need to eat. The time may come when you can't put anything in your mouth at all, and then you know there has been a change, a deep change in what you are. Something dead is changed from what it used to be when it was alive, and you are changed in that way. You aren't dead but you are beginning to be dead. You feel strange, as though you are wearing yourself like a suit of smelly clothes. After you are dead, you are a corpse; before you are dead, you have a corpse; you're wearing it. It feels stranger and stranger.

They told her friend that the time had come when the food couldn't go down her throat. There was nowhere for the food to go; part of her stomach was still inside her but it was filled with other things; if they removed the things no stomach would remain. They said six of one, half a dozen of the other, and her friend agreed that, if it was all the same, doing something and doing nothing, it was better to do nothing because nothing is less invasive. Her friend sat at the table with her family members and talked to her family members while her family members ate food but her friend did not eat food, would never eat any food again, her mouth no longer served that function. Her mouth was part of the corpse she was wearing.

She had not been invited to eat at her friend's house since her friend stopped eating, so she did not know exactly what her friend did at the table. She did not know if her friend set herself a place at the table or if she sat in her chair at the table with nothing in front of her. If she set a place for herself at the table, did she put food on the plate and a fork on the napkin, or did she leave the plate empty or did she perhaps put some non-food item on the plate, like a thumb-sized cactus in a plastic pot? She thought putting food on the plate would be torture, because the smell of food makes you hungry, and her friend must be hungry all the time, except maybe the hunger had become inseparable from the nauseated feeling, and so hunger didn't make her want food in the way it made other people want food, it just made her sick. In that case sitting upright at the table would be torture even if there was no food on her plate, and besides she could smell the food from the plates of her family members, if she could still smell, which was far from certain. She might forget, if there was food on her plate, that she could not eat the food, even though she felt sick, even though her mouth was a corpse's mouth and her throat was cracking with the dryness, and with disuse; she would pick up the fork and put food in her mouth and then remember and have to spit out the food. Would something go wrong if she swallowed the food, even a little food? Would it lodge somewhere in her, sit on top of the things in her stomach and rot so the rottenness gassed inside her and the gas came up to her mouth and her nose and burned and stank until she went to see them and they snaked the food out of her? It would be difficult not to put anything in your mouth after so many years of putting food in your mouth, all kinds of food, whether you were hungry or not.

She wondered what she would talk about with her friend if her friend invited her to dinner. She would bring her friend something, a plant, not a cactus, for her plate, in case her friend sat there with the empty plate in front of her. You can't fiddle with a cactus, and her friend might appreciate having something to do with her hands while not eating at the table. She might want to fidget because she wasn't dead and she couldn't be comfortable; she was in pain; she felt sick all the time. She might need to fidget, to distract her-self from the pain, and Americans distract themselves by eating, but not her friend. She was past that. All of those things—being American, being a woman, being an American woman—those are temporary things, states you pass through on your way to something else. Phrasing it like that made it sound like a jour-ney, a spiritual journey, and she would phrase it like that to her friend if it came up at dinner; she would focus on the journey, not on the something else you get to, because the journey is an archetype, everyone believes in the journey, but people can't agree about the something else. Beliefs about the something else are personal and she didn't want to pry. Of course, she wondered what her friend thought, and it did seem natural to try and get her to talk about it. It did seem like it would be the natural topic. After all, her friend was an eyewitness. Her friend was so close to it; she was beyond almost everything that had made her who she was. What she said would not be personal. What she said would just be witnessing, not her pain and fear, but the pain and fear of it, the something else, the thing that filled her.

WELL

The human body is not a good place to store things, not if you want them to keep. If you want the things to spoil, then, fine, put them in the human body. Put a head of lettuce in your body, it will wilt in the heat, the cellulose will turn to slime. If your mother says, "I'm making salad," and you want to stop her, you want to stop your mother from making salad, run to the kitchen. Take the head of lettuce, put it in your body. There will be no salad. Inside it is wet and hot: wet and hot, but not so wet, not so hot that it will blanch the green beans your mother stemmed to toss with lettuce in the salad. The green beans will not blanch in your body, they will go soft and slick and brown along the seams and leak slime from their wounded tips. The mushrooms will grow quick cowls of silty brown mucus, they will shrink. She doesn't really want salad. No mother wants salad. Run out and buy your mother a steak, very fresh, very cold

meat on ice under glass. Ice and glass and crisp air—
that is how to keep a steak from spoiling. It is too
bad your brain is in your body. Brains should be kept
like steaks, on ice under glass, or like celluloid in salt
mines, or cabbages in cellars. They should be cool
and dry at all times.

Brains are dense like cabbages, lobed like grape-
fruits, gilled like mushrooms, layered like lettuces;
they are made of meat, like steaks. In the wrong
conditions they brown, they soften, they ooze, they
stink, they shrink, they spoil. Your body is the wrong
condition for your brain. It doesn't help to strap fro-
zen peas around your skull; inside your skull, it's still
hot. When your breath comes out, it's hot. Your breath
is always hot, it smells of decay. What do you expect,
given the conditions? What can you do, chew ice?

There were years when your mother chewed ice.
She sat in her room, in the dark, chewing ice. She
only left the room to refill the ice trays. She kept the
door locked. You had to stand in the hedge and look
through her window to make sure she was alive, and
even then you couldn't be sure. She could have been
dead but still composed—she looked dead but intact,
unmoving. Now she looks alive because she is always
moving, opening and closing drawers, pacing from
room to room, rubbing her hands on her thighs, on
her arms, shifting her weight from foot to foot, twist-
ing her hands with her hands; she never stops. Her

body looks intact, but inside she has decomposed. Everything has softened.

What can you expect, given the conditions? It takes more than chewing ice. Your mother's poor brain, in that heat, that wet heat: nothing will help. Her bones have gone soft. You can tear her skin with your nails. You can wad her up, make a ball. You need to wad her up, you need to make her stop. She's always moving. Her skin is always wet. She seeps from the head, from the lap. Why did you think your mother would keep? Her hands were cool, but her breath was hot. What did your mother want? She removed you from her body before you could rot. She left her brain inside her body. She knew it wouldn't keep. You should have taken it out, you should have taken her apart. Even now, the parts of you are spoiling in your body. Who will take you apart? You need to ask. You need to find someone and say, "This is what I want." It is too late for your mother. No one can save her. There are no salvageable parts. She has gone too soft. Wad her up. Make her small. Take the ball of your mother in your arms. Put your mother inside your body. Let her rot.

EXCULPATORY CLAUSE

The realization that my death could never be proved, forensically, to me, was at first a great relief; I'd long resented the foregone conclusion of my dying. Then I began to miss that certainty, irrational as it had been; I sorrowed, as we do when any great trust is broken.

TALKING POINT

Right now, tonight, you could stay outside; you could spend the night outside; you wouldn't die. Tonight isn't mild, but it isn't brutal. Tonight could be endured. You could endure it. This is a temperate zone. Humans have fat and hairs to keep them warm and they can hold in their urine and make a heat sink. Humans are ingenious and can climb into dumpsters, and the trash isn't cold or hard as the pavement, and dumpsters have lids that keep out the rain. You would do alright if you had to stay outside. You would do fine. At night you would sleep in the dumpster and during the day you would leave. You would crawl out. You would air out. A woman might even notice you. She might notice you sprawling on the street and feel strangely excited. She wouldn't stop to talk with you, but she would notice your blunt hands pale against your rummaged coat, your hard, strong hands, and noticing them would do something to the woman, make her breath stick in her throat for just a moment, and the smell of you, the thickness of the smell of you in the thick, warm morning, your body only half aired out, would make her clench her thighs. You would do fine, sprawling, women stepping over you, women pushing air down their throats, tensing their stomachs and asses, their skirts tenting over you as they stepped. If you stay outside, you'll do fine. Stay outside. You'll do fine. Why go inside? No one is waiting for you. No one is inside, waiting, looking out the window. No one is wondering, is he fine? No one wonders about you. You don't matter. No one feels attached to you. When you go inside and they see you, they know you, they know what to call you, there are a few things they say to you, but when they don't see you they don't say anything about you. They don't call to you. They don't remember you. If they see you, they'll remember you. Your name is in their brains, it's retrievable, your face is in their brains, it's retrievable, but they don't retrieve your name or face unless they need to, unless you're in front of them. Your name and face are disposable; your name and face have the quality of things that are disposable, your name and face have that cheap, common, off-brand quality, but because you keep going inside, they can't dispose of your name and face. They have to keep your name and face somewhere in their brains. They have to clutter up their brains. They have to keep retrieving these disposable things from their brains. Tonight it's raining but just a little and the dumpster has a lid. Hold in your urine and make a heat sink. You can wrap your arms and legs with newspapers. It's not unendurable. You can endure it. You won't die. There are broken bottles, but there are more tissues than broken bottles. The smell isn't good, but if the rain stops you can open the lid. You can begin airing out. Rain changes at dawn. Rain starts or stops around dawn. If it's raining, the rain will stop around dawn. You've seen the city at dawn, the brown light of the bricks, and the steam rising from beneath the streets, and the blinking, beeping vehicles of the street sweepers and the garbage collectors moving slowly through the streets, through the steam that billows from beneath the streets. It stops raining around dawn but the steam from beneath the street, from the vents of the buildings, from the vehicles, condenses on the metals of the city. It's always raining in the alleys beneath the air conditioners, beneath the fire escapes. It's always raining under the bridges. Keep the lid of the dumpster closed. It's dawn and it was raining all night and it's still raining. You don't need to air out. It doesn't smell good but it doesn't smell terrible. You can wrap your arms and legs with plastic bags. Plastic isn't permeable. The smell won't get on you through the plastic. You hear beeping. Light moves up the crack between the lid and the dumpster. Garbage collectors don't look in the

dumpsters before they use the trucks to compact the
trash. Whether it's human or not human doesn't factor in. They don't look. They don't ask, "Is it human?"
This is not a question they have about trash. The trucks
move slowly along the streets. People are waking
up. They hear metal on metal. The forks engage. The
blades move towards the rears of the trucks. People
hear popping. They hear whirring, clanging, screech-
ing. Hissing steam. High and low pitches. Banging.
Thumping. Upside down the dumpster lids hang open.
Everything falls out. It isn't raining anymore. It's wet
but not raining. You could be outside, airing out. You
could come down to ground level and let the wind
that comes off the river disperse the smell of your
breakfast. Right now, this morning, you still smell
like your breakfast. You are surrounded by the smell
of what you ate for breakfast. It's in your hair and your
clothing and on your fingers and in the grooves of
your teeth. Let the air move over you. Right now, it's
morning. The city smells like breakfast, steam billow-
ing up, water falling back down, stickier on your skin
than you remember, sweeter. You think: juice. Syrup
from a bag in a box, syrup pumped through the gun
into the cup, cup spilling over, juice moving up the
moving wall.

DEFENSE OF MARRIAGE ACT

Sometimes even the best women pretend to be men. It is socially expedient to do so in certain situations. The women pretend to be men until the situation is over. Sometimes they pretend for longer, so long that they get used to it and aren't pretending. Then they have to pretend to be women again. This creates confusion. We meet an exemplary woman, one of the very best women, and sooner or later we realize that she's pretending. She isn't for real, but whether she's a man pretending to be a woman, or a woman pretending to be a man pretending to be a woman, we can't be sure. If we could go back to the beginning and establish the facts, using testimonies and also photographic and documentary evidence, we might say, look here, she started out as a man or he started out as a woman, we might settle the issue, but in the beginning, there are parents and parents often pretend that their child is a man or a woman, and why not? In the beginning, their children really aren't much. They aren't men or women, they aren't stockbrokers or teachers or plumbers or store clerks, fathers or mothers, they're balls of warm meat, tubes of warm meat, chubby bundles of cytoplasm and diarrhea, and so their parents have to pretend. They pretend the cytoplasm is a little man or a little woman, like they had to pretend in middle-school with the eggs or the bags of flour, this is my child, he is... she is.... The parents call the cytoplasm by name, they try to connect the cytoplasm with names. Very short names are best. Frederick always seems wrong at this stage. Bartholomew, Jacquelyn.

My mother, Georgia, is one of the very best women, although she might be pretending. She told me the truth about my father, that my father is not a man. She told me my father is a sentient tree, a barely sentient tree, or an inert gas, or a coma patient, a lump under a sheet that doesn't need a name. She said I could pretend he was a man if I wanted. I could pretend he was anything, except a good woman. He wasn't. He wasn't ever. She was, my mother, a good woman. One of the best, one of the most believable. I never saw her otherwise. She said no matter what I had to keep in mind, there is a difference.

THIRD-PARTY

The woman turned to lie on her side in the bed. Her body turned in bed, but she didn't turn. She was looking at the ceiling. It had happened. Her body was on the side of her. She thought about her mother's first husband. He was Jewish, but also Zen, and sometimes he left New York City to meditate. You can't talk at the meditation center, but when you come back to the city you can talk. Her mother's first husband loved to talk. Once he told her that her mother was sexually normal, and she never forgot it. At first she thought maybe it meant her mother had no hang-ups, she was a healthy and engaged sexual partner, but that couldn't have been normal, not for a girl in the late fifties, even a bad girl, a wild girl ungently raised; maybe it meant her mother had the normal hang-ups, normal for the time and place, for her caste and class. Her mother's first husband told her, when you meditate, you realize that you are not two things, not a

body and a mind. You sit down in a large room. You sit
for hours, for days, for three days, ten days. Suddenly
it happens: You become aware of a sitting body. You
become aware of a mind. You observe the twitches of
the body, its muscular and chemical properties, and
you observe the patterns of thought in the mind. This
"you" is a third thing; it is separate from your body,
which is sitting, and your mind, which is thinking.
The woman has imagined sleeping with her mother's
first husband. She has wondered if that would be normal. Within small circles of friends, it is normal for
the friends to sleep together, to pair off and break up
and recombine, and sometimes circles of friends are
intergenerational and one of the friends has slept with
your mother and then you sleep with that friend. It's
most likely normal.

There is a small chance, though, that it is sordid, a
sordid thing to do, and maybe if she did it—slept with
her mother's first husband—the sordidness would go
into retroactive effect. Her mother could no longer
be considered sexually normal, having participated
in a sordid love triangle with her own daughter. The
woman did not know her mother's second husband,
but if she met him and slept with him—either know-
ingly or through some strange coincidence—if she
slept with *two* of her mother's three husbands, that
would not be normal. Her mother's third husband was
the woman's father. The woman loved her mother's

third husband more than her mother loved him, but that was definitely normal. A daughter's love for her father isn't like the love of a wife for her husband, or a son for his father. A daughter's love for her father is a third thing, a special kind of love with an almost vestigial quality, a hold over from primitive times, when there were no parents *per se*, just fathers who owned their progeny, who could keep or kill or marry off their progeny to serve any purpose. In those times it was normal: fathers owning daughters, keeping daughters by their sides to feed them and bathe them and anoint their feet in their old age and warm their beds. Everyone shared a single room, a single pot. There was no privacy, no nicety, between fathers and daughters.

If the woman slept with her mother's first husband, would he tell someone, someday, that she was sexually normal? Once when the woman was very young she slept with a man, a lyricist for a jam band that toured college campuses, a man who was fervent with words, and after they finished, he massaged her palm with his thumbs. She used her other hand to stroke his long hair. He put down her palm and began to tap a rhythm on her chest, a gesture that might have seemed absent-minded but instead impressed her as simple and exuberant. Then he caught up her hand again and said, "That was the *penultimate*." Of course the man (who was also very young) meant something positive, he meant *super ultimate,* he meant that he had enjoyed himself, that it had been wonderful, their fucking, the best fuck of his life. He was the sort of man who would say something like that, a positive, sensitive man whose sincerity she questioned, although he always behaved in accordance with his expressed intentions and his expressed intentions were mild and consistent, not to mention kind, generous, and flattering. As their acquaintance deepened, and with it, her suspicions, she began to worry more and more about her character. Why did she question the man's sincerity? Why was she always looking for the worst in people? What vileness in her did she want to see borne out in the rest of humankind? Why couldn't a man say she was the best of fuck of his life and mean it? But he did not say that she was the best fuck of his life. He said of their fucking: that was the *penultimate*. And penultimate does not mean super ultimate. It means second to last. After she broke up with the man and did not find a new man, not immediately, not for years, she grew obsessed with what he had said regardless of what he had meant by it, which anyway she would never know for sure. *That was the last but one.* She wondered if part of her trouble finding a new man was the fear that he would be that: the last, the last one. She would break up with the man or the man would break up with her and she would never have another. Maybe that was why she now slept with so many, why she cheated on so many men, every man that she dated.

As soon as she slept with a man she needed to know that he was not the last, that there were more men, that she would never run out of men and lie for hours, for days, for months, for years in a bed with no one beside her to hear if she breathed. Was this normal?

She wanted to sleep with her mother's first husband so he would tell her. His last trip to the meditation center had focused on the meditations that you do to prepare for death. You go through cycles of dissolution as you die and you meditate through these cycles, until the last cycle, which is an aperture you enter with nothing on the other side. She lay in bed with her body turned over. She was not meditating, had never meditated, but something had happened. Her body had turned around her in bed, but she had not turned with her body. She was on her back, looking up, looking at the ceiling through her body, her rotated body. She tried to listen for her breath. Not her breath, the breath that moved in and out of her face, her face that was now on her side, to the left of her. She tried to listen for breath, to listen leftward. When you meditate you listen for your breath. You focus on your breath. Who is this you? Not her body. Not her mind. Who is this you? There is no one else in the bed. If she could talk she would say: Tell me. Tell me what's happening. Is this normal? But she can't talk. She can observe her thoughts. She observes them, they are moving. They are moving so quickly. They are turning around her.

Her body has stilled. Between, that might be an aperture. There is an aperture. Am I breathing? She would say: am I breathing? Between breaths, is that a widening aperture? Is that breathing? Who can tell you? It's part of breathing, not breathing. Her not breathing, it's the last part of the breathing. She's breathing. She's breathing. It's so wide, the black bed. She would tell him what it's like, what happens, how you listen, how you can't find your face.

MANUFACTURED
OBSOLESCENCE

A bat flew into the windowpane. At first the woman couldn't tell it was a bat—the impact happened too fast, and she was thinking of something else, sitting at her desk and thinking, the light from the window on her face, her eyes unfocused, so that she did not distinguish anything in front of her at any of its points— but then the impact came again, something folding and unfolding, a thin dark line suddenly widening, and she saw it was a bat, a bat reeling up and flying forward into the windowpane and on its next pass it slipped between the windowsill and sash and flew into the room. The woman ducked, then ran with her head down, ran out of the room, slamming the door, trapping the bat inside the room. She stood in the hallway on the other side of the door. She sat down in the hallway with her back against the door. She stood up, faced the door, and flung it open. She was breathing hard and flinched several times before she became certain that the bat was not flying toward her. She took a step inside the room. She surveyed the white corners of the ceiling and the bare curtain rod above the window and the narrow top ledge of the picture frame on the wall. She didn't see the bat. The bat must have flown inside the closet. The woman gathered herself. It was a false start. Her chest hurt her. She gathered herself. She ran forward and slammed the closet door. The bat was crawling over the dresses in the closet. The woman sat at her desk. She was breathing hard. She was thinking; her eyes were unfocused, but she was seeing. She was distinguishing dark and light points. She saw movement out of the corner of her eye. She flinched, but it wasn't anything. It was space. Behind space there is nothing more that is given. The woman sat at her desk. She embodied a volume of space. Her body was enclosed by a volume of space. She was facing it but it was also behind her. It was there in the closet. She could let it out of the closet but it was already beside her. It was inside her. She saw it again, moving. The dark line. It was her hand. It was the corner of the room. It was glass in the window. She was seeing it see her. She would crawl under the desk. She would stick her thumbnails in her eyes. She would back away from it slowly, so slowly she would hardly be moving. She would stop and let it pass over and through her and by.

TERMINATOR

The first night in her new apartment she decided to try out the shower. She took off her clothes and piled them on the lidded toilet. The floor was cold and there were mop streaks, straight, dark lines that made thin angles on the white tile. Sponge mop. She said, "sponge mop" aloud. She stepped over the rim of the tub. She stood in the tub. The former tenants had left their shower curtain liner. They hadn't put the rings through every hole. The liner sagged from the shower rod, filmy and white, bunched on one end of the tub. She didn't touch it. She examined the shower taps and the tub faucet. A brown stain ran down from the faucet to the drain, thicker on the tub wall below the faucet, thinning as it approached the drain. She looked on the rim of the tub for a stopper. No stopper. She didn't turn the taps. She looked around the bathroom. The bathroom was rather small. The bathroom was notably small. She noted it. What a small bathroom.

From her position in the tub, she could lean over and touch the toilet, the pedestal sink, the heating pipe, the door. She imagined white tiles on the walls. She imagined tiling the walls, outfitting the floor with a drain, using the entire bathroom as a shower, like in prison. She imagined the toilet glistening, water sluicing across the lid, down the porcelain slopes of the bowl, which would be metal in prison, a metal toilet, tiles on three planes of the room and the fourth plane, no tiles, a steel door with a slot. In prison, the toilets don't have lids. The water from the shower floods the toilet bowl and the water runs across the floor, across your feet, into the drain. The shower fixture is centered in the ceiling above the drain and there are settings that only the guards know how to change, one that switches the water from hot to cold and one that switches the water from liquid to gas. She has never been inside a prison. She has been to the Tower of London. She has been on a slave trade tour. They call them Heritage Tours if you are a black American but she is not a black American. She was in college. She does not remember very much about the tour. There were several sites. She remembered the van stopped at a rock. It was a large rock. When the tour guide was questioned about its historical significance he evaded the questions. He responded but his responses didn't make sense. His English was clumsy. His eyes were bright red. It seemed possible that the rock had no historical significance. There was something strange about the stop. An empty road. An empty plain. A large rock. What could have happened there? The tour guide would not say. The tour group got out of the van. The day was hot, like always. In Africa every day was so hot. It was the hottest day. People milled around the rock. She stood by the van. She smelled petrol and dust and the strong smell of the tour guide and the driver, the Africans. The driver wore mirrored sunglasses. He squatted by the van. The tour guide said something to the driver in French. He said another thing to the driver in an African language. A member of the tour group shouted to the tour guide from nearer the rock. He asked a question about the rock. The tour guide responded. He didn't shout. He mumbled. His eyes were red. She thought he said, "From here they go into the rest of the world." What did that mean? She wondered if the tour guide had an ulterior motive for stopping. She felt a pang, a sharp pang that ran through her whole body, as though her veins were stiffening, as though she had wires in her veins. She felt like an animal, scenting danger, no, sensing danger, with her blood. Her blood had reacted with something in the air, some danger. Something was wrong. Sun glaring on dust. Stillness. She met the tour guide's red eyes. For a moment, she could not repress images. It was a vision: men coming out from behind the rock, red-eyed African men in filthy t-shirts, with guns, forcing her to kneel, every member of the tour group kneeling behind the van, in the wheel ruts, the tour guide looking on, his red eyes. Her blood hurt everywhere. She panted. She couldn't get enough oxygen from the air, the thin, hot air. It was so still. The air didn't move. She tried so hard to get the oxygen inside her. She panted. The images kept coming. They were happening just in advance of the event, a hairsbreadth of predictive potency hovering between the vision and reality, the instant in which the men would emerge. If she could switch off the images, the men would not emerge. There would be nothing behind the rock. She saw herself kneeling in the line, an African moving down the line, stopping behind each member of the tour group, putting a bullet in the back of each head. The kneeling bodies tipped over one by one. He moved down the line. The gun reached the back of her head. She tipped over. She blinked rapidly; she jerked, trying to stop the images, but she saw herself on her knees, the African moving down the line, the gun at the back of her head, the body tipping over, as though she were standing behind the African, looking beneath his lifted arm with the gun. She was standing in plain view of the other Africans, and they were shouting to each other, pointing at her with their guns, coming at her, the waving guns steadied and they fired. They fired into her face and chest and the bullets that didn't hit her kept moving over the plain, farther and farther away from the van and the rock and the bodies between the van and the rock. Part of her moved with the moving bullets, and part of her was dragged forward; they dragged her forward so that she lay on top of her body in the wheel ruts—all the liquids from all the bodies were flooding the wheel ruts—and every time she tried to stop the images they started over again in sequence, the images stuttering, the men emerging and emerging, and she was always watching, every time they shot her she was still there watching, behind the bodies, farther and farther away from the van and the rock and the bodies, but the bullets didn't stop, they came at her, they burst her skin, embedded in her spine, they ripped through her soft tissues, they went out and out and out across the plain. She remembered that part of the tour. Finally, she had crouched in the shade of the van and drunk heavily from her water bottle, bright yellow purified water that tasted like plastic. The best policy was to drink as little as possible. She remembered pit latrines, the flies pelting her ass, their big, buzzing bodies wedging briefly between her thighs. It was shocking. Other times the van stopped at old slave markets. People were selling things, not inside the old slave markets, but near enough. She refused to buy anything. She wanted a few things, beads, cloths, but she wouldn't buy them. She would have felt uncomfortable, a white American, buying things, from Africans, right there,

near a slave market. She couldn't do it, not after hearing the stories she'd heard and now couldn't remember, and so she didn't buy anything from the Africans,
but that was wrong too, she knew it was wrong, Africans are poor, it would have been better to buy things,
to give back, to return money to Africans to make up
for the Africans that were taken, but slave-traders
paid good money for the Africans that were taken,
they bought the slaves, and this would be paying
again, buying the slaves all over again, she would be
participating in the slave trade, it was wrong, she
knew it was wrong, she couldn't. She thought maybe
her money should have gone to the black Americans.
Black Americans were standing all around her near
the market taking pictures, but she couldn't have
handed her money to a black American, the black
Americans weren't selling anything. What would they
think she was buying? She touched the shower curtain liner, pulled it towards her, enclosing the tub. She
turned the taps and lifted the lever for the shower.
Water came from the showerhead, not in drops, in a
mist, a fine, warm mist. The showerhead looked old,
slightly flared, discolored metal pipe. Fumbling at the
metal, she detected no settings, no way to intensify
the stream of water, to make the showerhead dis-
charge drops instead of mist. If there was a setting
someone else controlled it. Not guards. The building
manager. The landlord. A setting in the basement,

near the water heater. She couldn't change the way the water came out of the showerhead. Not there, in her bathroom. No matter where she stood, no matter how she positioned herself beneath the showerhead, it was as though she were standing next to the water, as though the water was falling nearby. She couldn't close the distance between herself and the falling water, although she was certainly getting damp. Her body was getting very damp. Her hair was not yet damp. She had coarse, dry hair that wicked away moisture. She tried to stand in the water, in the middle of the water, the dead center of the water. She knew there was water nearby. The mist made drops on her skin. She had often thought it would be terrible to fall beneath a truck, a big truck, a truck with a body's width of clearance from the road. She would not be crushed. She would be dragged perhaps, there would be glancing blows from prominences on the undercarriage, the differential girdle or the muffler or the shocks, there would be the slaps of the mud flaps, she would have to stay in the center, stay between the wheels, stay flat, face turned to the side, mouth open, screaming into the rushing dark, everything shaking, wet and hard, her clothing unraveling, her flesh laid open on the pavement, smeared at certain points of contact with the pavement, but the truck would keep going, she would not be completely crushed, there would be no definitive moment of impact, she would pass through between the truck and the road, she would come out the other side, face up on the road. The shower was like that, that awful, that feeling of being surrounded, and being spared.

LEFT BEHIND

After you clean, look around. The apartment is clean. It should be clean. You've been cleaning all day. You've been cleaning on your hands and knees. Did you degrease the back splash? The back splash is degreased. Good for you! You don't miss a trick. In the day to day, you are not the cleanliest person, but you apply yourself assiduously to tasks. Today you have cleaned assiduously. Are there fingerprints on the switch plates? No prints. Your work is done. You can leave. The blinds are dingy but blinds are always dingy. You can't clean a blind. How can you clean a blind? Should you walk the blind through the car wash? The car wash chemicals would kill you. They'd dissolve your clothes. The next driver driving through would find you dead on the ground inside the car wash, covered by a blind. The driver would feel like he was looking through a window, watching a naked girl through her window, but the girl is dead in the car wash. He'd feel like a dirty old man, a dirty peeping old man, and this would humiliate him; it would cause damage above and beyond the normal wear and tear you'd expect from discovering a body. There's nothing to do about the blinds. You can't kill yourself. The roach powder is getting into your brain. Get out of here! Leave. The blinds don't matter. You can leave. You have fulfilled the terms. You don't feel fulfilled, but, formally, there is fulfillment. The terms required you to do certain things, and there was a specified duration, and you did the things and this is the final hour of the duration. You can leave, even though you feel unfulfilled. You crawled on your knees with a toothbrush rubbing at the speckled linoleum. Some of the specks are dirt but some of the specks are manufactured in the linoleum to look like dirt. The fake dirt disguises the real dirt. It's impossible to tell the specks apart. You had to scour every inch of the floor. Now the floor is clean. You look at the floor. It doesn't look clean. The linoleum was manufactured with specks of dirt. The carpet is the color of dust. The bathtub is the color of stool. No one will believe you cleaned all day, on your hands and knees, the cracks in your skin stinging with degreaser. No one will believe you fulfilled the terms. You shouldn't have bothered. You will be blamed for the dirt and dilapidation, for the discoloration. Chips and stains. You will be blamed for the specks in the linoleum. You will be blamed for the condition of the carpet, of the bathtub, of the blinds, of the counters, the cabinets, the oven, the sinks, the water, the wiring, the plumbing, the gas. You will be blamed for the layout, the north facing windows, the dry air, the way sound travels up from the street. You shouldn't have spent the day on your hands and knees. You shouldn't have put your face so close to the floor that roach powder went into your nose. Where is your self-respect? You shouldn't have cleaned. You should have disguised the dirt with more dirt, more and more dirt. There's soil outside, not close by, but you could have walked a few blocks to a park. You could have brought back a baggie of dirt. Why didn't you go to the park? Then you'd have dirt. You'd have fresh air in your lungs and a baggie of dirt. Your thoughts would be clear. There's no poison in the park. There's no powder. You should have gone to the park. You should have come back with dirt. You should have packed the garbage disposal with dirt. You should have smashed a hole in the wall. It's not too late. Call your brother. Say you feel unfulfilled. Say you feel like a dupe. You've discovered that the apartment is dirt. It's made of dirt; every part is dirt, or lint or dust or stool or powder. If you get on your hands and knees, you get the apartment all over you. All day you've been getting covered in apartment. You've been rubbing and rubbing because there are terms and now your knees are stinging, your nostrils are rimmed with roach powder, you've got blood around your cuticles, but nothing is clean. You're surrounded by filth. You're in a box of filth. A toxic box. There are terms, but what can you do? Call you brother. He'll come right away. He'll come prepared with hammer and mackerel. There's a knock at the door. It's your brother. Look at your brother. Look at his skin, his darkly ringed eyes, the dark wings of his nose. Your brother looks like you. He doesn't ever look clean. Take the hammer. Take the mackerel. Smash a hole in the wall and stuff in the mackerel. Spackle the wall. Spackle over the mackerel. Spackle more patches than just the patched-over mackerel. Disguise the mackerel patch with haphazard patches. Now you can leave. You can live with your brother. He didn't come out of nowhere. There must be someplace to go.

NEIGHBORHOOD WATCH

I don't speak any English, but I quote from the English speakers copiously. They've said such staring things; I don't wonder they take notice of what I write down. It's English, what I write, and so they understand it, even admire it. English is an athletic language, and athleticism has had an erotic fascination for thousands of years. I don't think English has been around for thousands of years--from what I understand it's a young language, and its youth is the source of its vigor and appetite. I wish that I had learned English, on the playground, that's the place to learn a language, or in bed, that's the other, but now it's too late. When I go to playgrounds, the children won't teach me. But I enjoy the smell of tar and cedar and rubber and cold or hot metal and I enjoy sitting on benches, breathing the smells and watching the children, so I go to the playgrounds; I go to the playgrounds instead of scouring indoor sectors—restaurants, gyms, and shopping centers—for an English-speaking lover to take to my bed. I cannot pick an English-speaking lover from amongst the children on the playground; it is not permissible. I cannot take a child to my bed. To my home perhaps, that is permissible, for grape jelly and crackers and an exchange of lessons—the child would teach me English and I would teach the child how to stuff and roast a chicken—but children are not taken to bed in the English language, as English-speaking lovers. No, they are tucked into bed; they are brushed and scrubbed and then tucked into bed, by English-speakers who hush the children jealously. It's just as well I don't speak English. I am more classically disposed and prefer quotation to direct speech. Quotation is authorized and direct speech is plagiary. I do believe in the rule of law. I do believe in the orthogonal frame of the jungle gym, the children crawling over and through it, opening their mouths up wide, emitting sounds too high for my ears to register, and so I put the writing tablet on my thighs and transcribe vibrations which are hardly English, an English speaker could not read them, although the parents might see a family resemblance and warn their children to keep their mouths closed, touch nothing, remember the word that means I was sent for you, you can come with me, I will get you there safely.

BACK TO THE FUTURE

The bodyguards wear white. The bullets fly towards them. The bodyguards are clouds. The bullets do not penetrate Gaddafi. The bullets are precipitation. After we drink coffee, we check the bird feeders. Gaddafi has purple martins on his shoulders. The bodyguards are snowy egrets. Forget in both directions from this moment. I am right in front of you. I have a rifle. I am sexually wonderful like a horse.

PUBLIC EDUCATION

Children who learn Latin are not obese. Sometimes their eyesight is failing. Sometimes they are struck on the back of the head by tethered balls. Sometimes they are struck on the back of the head again by tethered balls. Sometimes they are struck on the back of the head again and again, always by tethered balls. Children who learn Latin like dogs. Children who learn Latin are cured of childhood diseases by non-therapeutic doses of penicillin. They succumb readily to poison. Often they are drowned by fluids in their lungs. Sometimes they are drowned in fresh water. They never drown in the sea. When children who learn Latin travel across the plains to the mountains, which are a basin-and-range formation, they have been known to slip on the scarps, the scree on the scarps. They have been known to slide all the way down from the range to the basin, and sliding, their skins rasp away. The ligaments pull from their bones and parts of their bones move violently to the surfaces of their bodies.

Long ago there was a sea, a sea where the children who learned Latin lie looking at parts of their bones. The ripples of water are preserved above them in the rocks, among traces of aquatic worms. I could not drown this way, in strong sunlight on alluvium, looking at parts of my bones, but I did not learn Latin. Children who learn Latin are not afraid to die. Hiking, I have gathered their broken glasses into specimen bags. I have separated rims, hinges, temples, lenses into specimen bags. Beyond the outcropping, the butterflies remain unlabeled, sorting themselves by color on the flowers. I am very afraid.

AGE OF MAJORITY

I have not had sex in many years but my gay friends assure me that were I to have sex, even one time, there would exist the possibility of a resulting pregnancy carried successfully to term. Because, my gay friends point out, I would have the sex with a man. If the sex involved the method conventional to people like me, that is, my gay friends specify, people with vaginas who use their vaginas at least occasionally for sex with men, then my vagina would be penetrated by the penis of the man, repeatedly, because the repetition of penile motions in the vagina is exactly what people like me define as "sex," even though my gay friends have mentioned alternatives. If a man took the teleological view, which he would (say my gay friends), he would, of course he would, he would attempt to use the sensations he derived from the penile motions in my vagina to produce orgasm, ejaculating in or near my vagina, thereby terminating the sex act as such, according (continue my gay friends) to the masculinist teleology of sexual conventions observed by people like me in our present society. Did you finish? Did you finish? Would he ask me that? Maybe, they concede. Maybe the man would ask me that.

But I would lie; I would say, "Mmmmmhmmmm" (say my gay friends). I would use the convention of murmurous assent so that the man could get on with his nocturnal commitments, dog walking, sleeping, or watching recorded sports footage, what have you. If the man were having difficulty ejaculating, because of some blockage, or because he was nervous or because he took a pill, perhaps a selective serotonin reuptake inhibitor or a non-selective serotonin reuptake inhibitor, I would feel that I had failed in my function as a woman, because, explain my gay friends, I am affected by the pressures in our present society that correlate a woman's value as a woman with her ability to satisfy the sexual desire of man, even a man for whom she feels no strong attachment. My ego would drive me to little tricks—perhaps pelvic floor contractions and exaggerated moans—and the man would eventually ejaculate, ending the sex act by the standards established by our present society and possibly fertilizing an egg, which I might decide to gestate, having developed a psychic connection with the egg, for either hormonal or emotional reasons (although it is unlikely that such a fine distinction is possible to make), and finally I would be delivered of one, two, or three humans. Could I claim that they consented, these humans, these new humans held up into the cold air, howling?

No, I could not, I could not make such a claim. Every being is born in this way, every being is born unconsenting—that is what I would say, say my gay friends. The being is made by violation. Before the violation, it doesn't exist. Humans make humans, I would say. It is what we make of non-Being. More and more humans, born to die, unconsenting. And I would be okay with that, they say. I would be perfectly okay.

PUBLIC POLLING

Ask your boyfriend what's worse, to play your birthday in the lottery every week your whole life and lose, or never to play the lottery at all—you never ever play the lottery—and one day your birthday hits and you don't win anything. If your boyfriend says, how would you know your birthday hit in the lottery if you don't play the lottery, only people who play the lottery pay attention to the numbers that hit in the lottery, then he is not a good boyfriend. He is poison. He is trying to control you. Every day he's taking one of your socks and leaving a rock in the drawer, a bottle cap in the drawer, a sweatshirt cord, a razor, a pencil lead, a blank check with a woman's name and address in the top left corner, a woman you've never heard of. He wants to make you feel weak and frightened. He wants to make you feel crazy. He moves the bookmark in your book every time you put it down. Sift flour on the bookmark, dab it with cellophane tape, you'll see; his fingerprints are all over it. You have to be a detective to live with a boyfriend like that. You have to anticipate his next move. You have to glue the bookmark in the book or you have to replace the bookmark with the thinnest package of UV ink, marking ink. Put the package between two pages you've already read, because when it explodes, the pages will be covered with ink, your boyfriend's hands will be covered with ink, and the smoke he inhales will dye his tongue blue and he will spot his lips with the tip of his tongue. If your boyfriend says, it's the same thing to play the lottery and lose and never to play and not to win, there's no difference, either way you get nothing, then he is not a good boyfriend. He is violent. He slams on the brakes in the car, he bangs on the steering wheel in the car, he bites the steering wheel and he looks ugly as a stoat, growling and drooling, shaking his head from side to side with the steering wheel deep in his mouth, between his back teeth, and you laugh and he stops biting with his lips slack and wet, stretched out, and he tells you to get out of the car, get out of the fucking car. Or he slams on the brakes in the car and he gets out of the car, and he walks fast down the road. His feet go out far to the sides when he walks but his crotch goes straight ahead. His back is hunched so his crotch can go up higher, stick out further. What can you do with a boyfriend like that? You could hit him with the car. You could drive behind him slowly with the hazard lights on, crying, pleading out the open window, until he jumps the divider, crosses lane after lane. Then there's nothing you can do. Peel out, speed away, wait at the house. If your boyfriend says, obviously, obviously babe, it is worse never to play, you gotta try and try, even if you don't succeed, that's the name of the game, then he is not a good boyfriend. He is an idiot. He thinks women pee out of their vaginal canals. You can't explain it to him. He doesn't know what color your eyes are. He says you shouldn't feel bad, he doesn't know what color anyone's eyes are. He taps on your arm with his fingertips when you sit side-by-side. His eyes are blue, big and blue. If your boyfriend says, I did play your birthday in the lottery and it hit, your birthday hit and here's twenty million dollars, and he pulls the couch away from the wall and you see where he'd hidden the cardboard check, a check exactly the same size as the back of the couch, then he is a good boyfriend. He loves you enough to play your birthday in the lottery and win. No one who hears about this will ever forget your birthday again; you'll get texts from everyone you know on your birthday, texts that say LUCKY DAY smiley face surprised face wink wink palm tree hearts & diamonds!!!!!

Your boyfriend answers other questions correctly too. Ask him anything. Ask him what's worse, to outlive you, to live without you year after year in the enormous house, swimming laps in the pool, eating vol-au-vents alone by the pool, fit, darkly tan, getting older and older, failing slowly, or to die first, to die soon, rich and in love, to die right now. Ask him what's worse, fear or hope. Ask him to keep the twenty million dollar check, to carve a hole in it, to fuck you through the hole, once a year, on your birthday. Who needs twenty million dollars? Ask him what's worse, to press your skin against a person's skin, to touch on every piece of skin, and to feel where your body ends and to feel the body that's not your body outside of where your body ends, a thing you can never get to, a thing that doesn't exist, or not to press your skin against a person's skin, to put a sheet, a board, a cardboard check between your skin and the person's skin, and imagine that skin to skin you would finally know that other person and be known by that person, wholly known, and so you never touch that person's skin but strain towards it through the barrier you erected, longing for a thing that's there, right there on the other side. Ask him what's worse, killing or dying. If you do it together you have to do it at the same time, it has to happen at the exact same time, but there is a very big risk. If you try, you need to recognize that the odds are against it.

RELIGIOUS CONFLICT

Is Jesus a man or a thing? I recall some conflict about this. The Crusades, then I remember something about croissants, they pose a threat to Christendom, but that was centuries ago. Now all Parisians are Catholic. I am Catholic. There is the Father, the Son, and the Holy Ghost. Three things together are stable and strong. Look at the tripod. The tripod is stable and strong. Three people together are not stable or strong, though, it's the wrong number of people. One of the people is always left out, or the left out person alternates. Sometimes one person is left out, sometimes another person is left out, but one of the people is never left out. That person is God. A tripod can't be made out of people. It won't hold together. A tripod can be made of three things, or a tripod can be made of one person. Of course, a dead person is a thing. Is it the deadness of Jesus that was in question? After the scourging, after the nailing of the wrists to the patibulum, Jesus died faster than anyone expected. He cried out and the soldier pierced his side and he spurted blood and water and Luke, the doctor, couldn't find a heartbeat, and Jesus no longer breathed. Nowadays people talk about the brain. Death is the irreversible cessation of activity in the brain, but in the case of Jesus the cessation was reversed. He stood up in the grave, he came out of the grave. Without the use of his brain, he couldn't have spoken to Mary and Thomas, or climbed the mountain in Galilee, or gone swimming in the Sea of Tiberias. Jesus used his brain when he came out of the grave-- not immediately, but shortly after. The cessation of activity in Jesus' brain turned out to be reversible, and so he did not die, technically. He was never dead according to modern medical standards. Of course, it is proleptic to use modern medical standards when discussing the death of Jesus.

Are religious conflicts fought over prolepses? Prolepses are not tangible, like croissants. Could prolepses mobilize the children of France to march on Jerusalem? No, I don't think so. My father lost control of the right side of his body, and of language. We'd never claim that he has died, since half of his brain still functions, but there is no speaking, climbing, or swimming anymore for my father. He can eat a little broiled fish and honeycomb. He can move his tongue, his heart beats, he breathes. He sits in his chair facing the sliding doors through which he watches birds come to the feeder. He is necessarily left out of decision-making processes, leaving me, my brother, and my mother to decide how best to support him. The worst is when we startle the birds, and my father sits watching the empty feeder, the bare porch railing, and tree limbs—the doubt in his eyes.

POCKET DIAL

Rub your face on the pants of the man. Feel where he's hard. The man wants to fuck. Take off your clothes. Don't worry about your body. The man is not comparing your body to the bodies of other women he's fucked. He is not comparing you to women he wants to fuck from TV. The man is making a Gestalt of all of your bodies, all women's bodies. Your small tits are part of a pattern of tits. It's okay that they're small. The pattern is large. You are part of a pattern. Relax. Rub his pants. Rub your face on his pants. Look up from his lap. He's looking down at your face near his pants. Can you feel he's turned on? The light is harsh in the room. The light doesn't flatter your face, but don't switch off the light. You're not young, but factored in with young women, you're young. The sum is quite young. Remember he's seeing the sum. Remember it's not just you in the room. It's not just you who he'll fuck. What you should feel is relief. Kneel by the chair. Grab at his pants. Get rough with his pants. Lift up the fold. Lick the zipper and moan. Stroke. Don't withhold. You can't bend your back. Your hamstrings are taut. Your mouth is small and it hurts to open your mouth. Your jaw always cracks. So what? It's okay. The man doesn't care. Your body can't make all the right noises and shapes. That's why you have help. The man doesn't want you, but you are enhanced by all the women he wants. It's great. All the women are here. It's a gift. They are superimposed. Don't complain. Don't try to stand out. You look old. You look fat. Relax. Sit on his lap. It's so hard it's a shock. Don't be shocked. Grind your hips. Use your weight. Make it snap. It's okay. You can't worry what's what. You know who you are and you know what you want.

OCCUPY

My brother and I entered our barbarous phase—matted hair, girdles of pelts—and we lived alone together in culverts of the town. The houses of the town were still standing and some retained furnishings: credenzas from furtive raids—heavy, inscrutable credenzas—also beds and chairs. We dragged blankets to the culverts, cushions, tins of food, and tableware. I can't remember what principle restrained us from living in houses. The fear of corners, perhaps. Is that a principle? -We would not be caged. We filled hampers with bath mats and canvas shoes and dragged the hampers to the culverts. We made herbal teas over hamper fires and the herbal teas soothed us. We used the herbs at random. Certain herbs stimulate the nerves and passions, and certain herbs are soporifics; they dull the mind and body. Maybe we were dulled on herbs. Sometimes at night we couldn't agree on objects. The number of sides. We made a game of it. We slapped each other's hands. We were always hot or cold, and slept greedily. The culverts were dry. We scratched a tally mark each day in the dirt. We scratched more shapes and guessed at them. We never guessed right. Maybe we just changed our minds. Later we emerged; we sought out others to see what they did, how they desired. My brother played us and I played them. We were matched in our capacities for violence, cutting holes in dead time according to no procedure.

BAILOUT

Now that the son is grown and wants to move the parents into a smaller house, he needs to convince the parents—who are not incompetent, not in the legal sense of the word, but merely impractical, stubborn, dangerous, and very old—that a smaller house will be suited to their needs. They can manage and afford a smaller house, and they can't manage and afford the house they have. The son might say this to the parents, but he knows saying it would not convince the parents that they should move into a smaller house. The parents have never felt that need to afford or manage anything in particular. When they can't afford something, they do without it. Not only that, they *disdain* it. Who needs that thing? It's amazing, isn't it, how many things are available today that people really don't need? When the parents can't manage something, it blows up or falls apart or gets away from them. It creates a bad situation that either disappears on its own or doesn't, gets better or worse or stays the same. And so? The parents have survived innumerable bad situations—they've survived far longer than the son, who thinks life is supposed to be easy, that situations don't arise. The son can show the parents where their roof is leaking, where the stovepipe from the basement furnace glows orange and flickers with the black shadows of flames. He can talk about the rising cost of gasoline, the distance between their house and a supermarket, their house and his house, their house and a hospital, their house and another house, any house, a house where they can find help, reach help when they need help in haste. But the parents don't need help. That's what the son doesn't understand. The parents don't need the son. They did without the son before and they can do without the son again. They don't need each other. They don't need them-selves, not really. What selves do people think they're hanging on to anyway? Not their old bodies, their very old bodies? Who wants to hang on to a very old body, even your own? People remember being young and they think that's what they need, those selves, supple and strong, but they don't. They don't need them. Not really. Those selves are gone and people make do with-out them. Every day people have less of those selves, but they go on living. The parents do enjoy living. They enjoy puttering in the yard, feeding the birds, making late night pancakes, watching TV, and feeling warm inside the big, untidy, half-rotten house that the son can't convince them to leave. It's a death trap, a money pit, a pigsty, an eyesore, an outpost. It's more than the parents need. The parents need so little, though, it's unforgivable that the son would try to take that little bit away.

PYRAMID SCHEMES

One venal day, I was brought before the judge to answer for my crimes, property crimes, the reading out of which gave me no hope that the good men and women of the court would tremble as the bailiff marched me past. I had no chains to rattle, I found no fearful face upon which to train my baleful eye. The good men and women murmured behind their hands in the cadence of wives exchanging recipes. The judge was fresh from chambers and awaited me with a patient smile. When I arrived before him, his placid mien, a trifle waxen, changed not at all. Nothing impended; he did not intensify his presence, and if he scrutinized it was with such mildness that I mistook his scrutiny for the reflection of a mind in harmony with the workings of untroubled digestion, a spotless conscience, and an incurious nature unchinked by partisan feeling. He was content to sit and hear the story of my life, and the story of my life would not move him.

I was born the son of a surgeon, whose cut along the midline of a mistress not yet whimpering with her pangs has been called precipitous by some. For every surgeon's cut one can find detractors. I do not speak to that. I will say only that the consequences were unhappy. My mother died, and I presented from the first instant of my independence both an exquisite face and an intolerance of gratification delayed by even small degrees.

My father was a glacier—white gloves and mask and pale blue paper suit—and silent assistants circled him like terns. To stay awake and thus alive in those conditions, I learned the choreographies and could soon anticipate my father's moves. In fact, I was moves ahead, could slip a rongeur up my sleeve, before my father, poised to open windows in a skull, held out his hand. How the terns would wheel about, fanning through the room to converge again at the tiny table where they scrabbled the gleaming instruments! Were those my first thefts? Those minor disappearing acts? Altogether they constitute the unseen whoreson's only game.

From a single action all that accrues cannot be known within a lifetime or within any span of time unless we presuppose time's limit and arrive. I have other arguments, but I will let this one run its course.

Why not a career in surgery? I'm as fit as any insouciant youth who comes to the laboratory in his finest coat, red with pale pink piping, and stitches his lover's name above the hearts of cadavers. The night before I began my training, my father handed me an amber jar. The vapor that rose was caustic, the contents coiled, the coils luminous, preserved in a fluid that diffused their glow. "What do you see?" asked my father. When I did not answer, he took back the jar, drew his chair close upon the hearth, and spoke rapidly into the fire: "The makings of a deathless race, men undaunted by the cooling earth, the dimming sun, because their flesh gives heat and light and does not self-consume. We may practice our craft on bodies of woman, but we are pledged to the perfectible...." The next morning, I took a train to a dark lake and lived in solitude for seven months. When I returned even limbless beggars seemed intricate, and dazzled me.

I wasted no time and sought at once the unattended wagon, piled high with bloomy grapes. I seized a largish bunch and made my way with it into the market crowd. Though easy it would have been to surrender to the hurried throng, to lift my legs and let it sweep me through the stalls and spit me out into the green where I might have gone skipping under my own redoubled powers to the line of carriages and, choosing the carriage with the steel gray pair, handed the driver a thick card printed with an address fashionable, if not by reputation then by the lettering, and thus made certain my escape, disliking tumult as much as certainty, I pushed free and sat on the edge of a fountain,

dropping plump grapes into the water. Like the inno-
cent, grapes sink. Beggar children, laughing, diving
for the grapes, pulping them with their ugly heels,
were corralled by guards and loaded into a farmer's
wagon to be taken to the countryside. They sleep now
in hedges, growing fat on pears. I had enough coins
in my pocket to buy many grapes. Of course, I bought
nothing; what is at stake in those kinds of exchanges,
all things being equal? When I have grieved someone,
wronged him, entered into his debt, or given him a
gift that he cannot repay, these are the ties that chafe,
that bind, that make of us real persons.

I rowed a gondola through deep canals. The gondola
was very old and grand and wanted at least one other
man to row her. I invited no passengers, though several
widows in palace doorways followed me with accus-
ing eyes. It was a typical expedition: joyous, fraught,
and brief. I capsized as I angled left and caught the
tarred rope thrown by the authorities. I did not resist
arrest but did refute the charges that I had stolen the
gondola of Giancarlo Ferrara; it was the canal that I
had taken, its many channels and the quadrants they
divided, the homes and shops, hotels and palaces,
theaters and cathedrals, the whole moldering city,
every stone, every watery fathom, the citizenry, the
tourists and parasites, Giancarlo Ferrara, his wife and
his daughters, their lapdogs, marzipans, and books; I
let it be known that I had taken everything. Of what

import was one gondola, to me, even a grand one, in such an inventory of my possessions? What was one gondola, to them, in such an enormous catalogue of crimes? Small men hector with such details, but the great stand at a distance.

VOYAGER

My goat is sick. I have to put my goat down. First I
would like to memorize my goat. Oh goat, your gold
eyes. I stand with a feed can. This is old river-bottom
land, rocky and flat, with a milking shed and the final
gold hours of my sick-to-death goat, the sky a low
hood. My goat knows this gray liripipe through wet,
worn-down hills is old river bottom, cloud covered.
My goat roams as though freely. Should I recite the
hairs on my goat? I don't know the deep sequence. I
could donate my goat. Tell me what to know, in the
interest of science, in the open. Rain seen as rain,
which is wet in the air, a very old river. The bones of
my goat are already there, in my goat. A black stitch
in gold. My goat can no longer swallow the tree leaves.
Scattered branches, traced with frost in the river,
emptied from trees.

THE BEST OF BEES

My father goes to the pines. He checks on his hive, it is destroyed. The bear wrecked the hive. My father goes to his house. He paints his body with honey. He applies many coats. He goes to the pines. He goes to the wreck of his hive. He lies in wait for the bear on the wreck of his hive. He wears six coats of honey, six full coats. It smells like pines in the pines, like strong honey. Honey attracts. My father waits for the bear to attack, to come through the pines, to rush toward the honey-thick smell in the pines. My father will kill the bear with his hands. Every man wants to kill a bear with his hands. Every silly old man. My brother calls my father a silly old man. My father is old. He has no teeth, has no hair. He has very strong hands. The bear will rush through the pines. My father will smile. Surprise! He will put his hands on the bear. Even now he is preparing to choke out the bear. My brother has entered his prime. He's not a boy. He knows his own mind. He knows my father will fail. It's not hard to see: a silly old man, old hands, and a bear. My brother proposes an alternate plan. He'll spread tacks. He'll plant mines. "Come back inside," he yells, but my father does not respond to commands. He won't surrender the field. He is lying in wait, his toothless head in his hands. It's not hard to see: my father will die. This is the plan. My brother throws a grenade. It rips through the bear, but my low-lying father, my father is spared. He comes through the pines, through the smoke, covered in all that honey covered over with all the bear's hair. On his head, on his cheeks and his chin, on his chest and his legs, on the backs of his hands and the tops of his feet. My father looks young, a dark, hairy young man. He holds up his hands. He says, "That bear destroyed his last hive." He's alive. That's the plan. He comes out young and alive. My brother pretends he was nowhere nearby. He trims his black hair, he builds his own house from the pines, he feels too alone, then remembers that honey attracts. He paints his body with honey. He waits. Driving with the window rolled down, his future mate brakes. She smells pines. She smells something strong: warm caramel, red clover. She leaves the car on the side of the road. She walks to my brother's pine house where he's waiting outside. She sees ants thick as thieves on honey, but beneath the honey, she sees the shape of a man.

HUMANITIES

A little girl wanders in the woods and she finds a cottage and she goes inside through a pretty painted door set neatly on hinges and she sees a table set for three. The cottage doesn't smell like wild animals, even though it is the den of animals, because the porridge is hot in the bowls on the table, and the cottage smells like cinnamon porridge. The girl doesn't find the animals in the cottage. They must have left the cottage. They must have left suddenly, unexpectedly. The girl coming made the animals disappear like when the angel comes to make the world right and the angel dissolves bodies with flames. The girl creeps up to the table. The porridge is still hot. The porridge is too hot, too hot to put in her mouth and send down to her stomach. It burns her tongue and she can't taste the porridge, the butter and cinnamon, it hurts the skin on her tongue, the taste is gone from her mouth. She spits porridge on the tablecloth and she moves from place to place at the table. She blows on the porridge. The porridge cools. The girl eats from every bowl at the table. She gets her germs in every bowl. The girl is filled with germs that are not dangerous when they are inside girls, but when they crawl out, they are dangerous. They hide in the creases of raisins in porridge. Eating, the girl tastes her tongue. She notices the shape and taste of her tongue, because it hurts. Her tongue hurts but soon it hurts less. The girl is filled with porridge and the bowls are filled with germs on raisins. Everything is right. Everything is good. The girl spits in bowls. The animals have been dissolved by flames. Before this moment, things weren't right— the animals in the cottage, the germs in the girl, the girl in the woods, the raisins in the porridge—the world wasn't right. It was all a bad hazard. The sparrow-mouth beneath the bonnet formed words. Before she left, the girl heard: "Don't go." She heard: "More light than anything can hold." The girl ran out into the woods. Even the black hole—it cracks open. Before the girl reaches the cottage, her rays reach the cottage. When she meets them, there, at the threshold, she is old. The door is singed. The door bangs in the wind. She sees herself at the table, a little girl: rashes, sparse hairs. She stands at the door with the fire behind her and between the hot strokes come the cold. She feels the darkened limbs of the animals. They have come back. They have come back through the flames. There are animals behind her, stroking, and she screams with a sparrow mouth through the door. The germs eat the light. The girl wears her bones outside of her skin. The cottage will fall. It will fall. It cracks open. I am not afraid. The slope of the ceiling touches the floor on one side of my attic bedroom; there is no wall there. Nothing can blow the wall down.

AGE DEFYING COVERAGE

My mother liked to tell me about a certain kind of young newly married person. She would not say "girl" because she did not want to make light of the marriages of the dead and a married person, although dead, could not be considered a girl, not in the way that I was a girl, an unmarried, maybe never married girl, but "married woman" would not do, because this type of young, newly married person was certainly not a married woman, not the way my mother was a married woman, a married woman who gave everything to her marriage, who didn't hold a single thing back, no secret resource, and so was entirely married, a real woman really married, unlike these newly married persons who would give fifty percent of what they had to their marriages and expect fifty percent back, so that marriage became an exchange of half-measures, perfect for a person who did not want to love or suffer like a woman, who did not want to give her all, for all or for nothing.

My mother divided this kind of young, newly married person into two groups. The first group went jogging. They were always jogging, up and down the roads, and men would stop their cars on the shoulders of the roads and follow them behind a tree in the cow field or they would just sink down right there together in a leaf pile. "That's jogging," said my mother. The second group wore linen and set strict limits on the use of the television. My mother liked to tell me about a member of this group who once tried to make my mother eat fruit-juice-sweetened biscuits that she was also feeding to her dog. "She thinks her dog's shit smells like fruit juice," said my mother. "Because of the biscuits. But does that explain the smell of the biscuits?"

Luckily, this certain kind of young newly married person that my mother liked to tell me about didn't last very long; she filled up with cancer, or hit a moose with her car, and she died, not always young in years but not old like my mother who tells me she will live forever, old as the day she was born.

PERMAFROST

It is time for the son to leave the parents, not because the son is as old now as the parents were when they brought the son into the world—although many believe this is the age beyond which a son cannot stay—and not because the son has found someplace else to go— there is only one home for a son—but because the first snow of winter has fallen and this year the parents have decided to crawl out into the snow—on a night with strong moonlight, crawl out into snow—and between the apple trees roll onto their naked backs and move their limbs back and forth, back and forth, and then stop, stop moving their limbs, and lie still in the snow and look up—at the moon, at ice on apple boughs lit up by the moon—and speak a few words to each other that the son should not hear.

BABY BOOMERS

This woman's father ended in the usual circumstances, hands gripping the bed rails, nurses hurriedly switching off the overhead television to create a more pregnant moment, etc. This woman shortly after cleaned out her father's house with the help of the son of her father's friend from church. She let him take the guns and armchair and dispose of the foodstuffs, dishware, and clothing. She retained at his suggestion booklets of coins, cigar box of watches, the albums, wedding ring, letter opener, and model train. She agreed to sell what tools he didn't want himself, and the mower. He seemed interested in the garage, and she gave him keys so he could return whenever he wanted to sift at his leisure.

Once, this woman paid the son of her father's church friend particular attention. She became aware of him before she became aware of other people in a room. Cleaning out her father's house, she did not feel particularly aware of the son of her father's church friend. She would forget he was in the other room, or walking over to where he knelt boxing up slippers to proffer her father's candy dish of licorice allsorts, she would notice, as though for the first time, an old poster on the wall, the baseball player on the dugout steps, and this baseball player, eyes washed out into the gray scale of the squidgy face, was a man whose presence demanded mustering, a man who attracted and returned her gaze.

Why wouldn't this woman think, after her father's house had been cleaned out, that she had finished with her father and with her father's church friend's son? There could have been one reason only: that she did not think at all about being finished or not finished.

This woman received a year after her father's death a phone call from the son of her father's church friend. He said he had waited a year out of respect for the dead to communicate what he had to communicate. This woman held the phone carefully. She had a good demeanor on the phone, her tone warm and direct but dimmed by the respect she had for the mediating apparatus, making no attempt to contrive immediacy. The son of her father's church friend told her that her father had been a Nazi sympathizer. What her father's sympathies amounted to, spiritually, was not for the son of her father's church friend to say, but he had recovered from her father's garage records of financial contributions as well as notes from the meetings her father had attended, and so she could gauge her father's commitment to the Nazi cause in terms of monetary support and hours invested if she desired to make that reckoning with the records the son of her father's church friend would shortly make available.

This woman observed an appropriate pause.

The son of her father's church friend said that his own father was also a Nazi sympathizer, which is why he had known what to look for in her father's belongings. The son of her father's church friend did not have as good a demeanor on the phone as this woman. He had an unctuous phone voice, and she disliked the way he insinuated that an intimacy pertained between them, as though they were bonded, direct products of their fathers' shared sympathies.

This woman began to receive grubby two-color pamphlets in the mail from a group called *Adult Children of Nazi Sympathizers*. She suspected that the pamphlets were printed on the Risograph in the basement of the church that she, her father, her father's church friend, and her father's church friend's son had once attended. The pamphlets made the case that Adult Children of Nazi sympathizers were Not Alone. In fact, the language of the pamphlets was so inclusive that this woman wondered if the entire population of her city was comprised of Nazi sympathizers and their kin, and what might account for that, if her city was exceptional among American cities, or if other cities were also populated by Nazi sympathizers. Or perhaps the pamphleteers employed a liberal definition of "Nazi sympathizer," with no evidentiary hurdles; people were free to dredge their own hearts for the precipitate of an instant's libidinal complicity. Would this woman find it, that black sediment? Hadn't this woman stared at photographs—mountains of corpses—and held herself aloof, alive outside the frame, unable to identify with the mounded victims, their imponderable fate? Hadn't she then identified with something else—with the life that prevailed, the victor, the triumph of all blood that ran hot and dark, not yet stilled?

This woman had never before encountered the phrase "Adult Children" and it shocked her. She found a bedbug in the fold of one of the pamphlets, and so she stored the pamphlets in a freezer bag in the freezer. On Sundays, when the mailman would not come and she knew she would receive no additional pamphlet, she removed the freezer bag and sat with it at the table. She inspected the pamphlets, their haloed lettering conferring status, using her teeth to pull cold banana rounds from the tines of a dessert fork. This woman was quiet, stable, and she labored. She kept herself, her dog, and her house free of filth. She made no unreasonable demands on her acquaintances and she did not acquaint herself precipitously with anyone, unreasonable or otherwise. She ate no candy, not even licorice. Her bust was static inside her blouse, a mono-lith, impervious, massy; it quelled vibration. She was brisk and frugal. She did not cry. She did not shriek, giggle, slur, lisp, interrupt, or forget her manners.

This woman would sit in the hard chair at the table, never kicking the chair legs. What if this woman was not a woman, but the child she had put behind her, that same child, adult now and underfoot? This woman would return the pamphlets to the freezer and pack the dessert fork and Tupperware into the dish-washer. She would drive briskly to the grocery store and then home again.

This woman did not have a favorite day of the week, but if she did, of course it would be Sunday, which somehow is the largest, emptiest of days. The other, smaller days try to piggyback upon it, but Sunday is too round. The other days slide off and lie curled up in a row, the ones past and the ones to come, like dead leaves or monkeys' paws or brown insects on the pale, blue field.

FOXHOLES

When people come to a door they knock on the door. They wait before they try the knob. If you are behind the door, you have time to look through the peephole. You can consider the people. A peephole is most often in the center of a door. Most people come to a door and stand directly in front of the door. They knock on the center of the door from half an arm's length away. Some peepholes are set near the left edge of the door. A peephole set near the edge of a door is for seeing the people who stand off to the side when they knock. These are the people who think they might have the wrong door. They lack confidence, in themselves, or in the situation. Their knocks are glancing, coming from too far away, from an angle too oblique. These people aren't sure who will come to the door; they aren't sure they want to encounter that person; it might be a bad idea. It might be awkward, unpleasant, or inconclusive; it might become tearful or violent, the encounter;

it might be better aborted. The people who stand to the side of the door when they knock are ready to run, are ready to spring at the person who opens. They could go either way. The sound of the turning bolt could decide them. In the door to my new apartment the peephole is set near the left edge of the door. I had been accustomed to a centered peephole. Now that I am getting used to my apartment door, I think it makes sense that peepholes would be near the edges of doors. It makes sense, when you hear the knock, to look for the half-hidden people, the hesitant, aggressive people, and so it makes sense to set peepholes near the edges of doors, although a peephole near the edge of a door only shows you the people who stand on the side with the peephole. Every hallway allows approach from two directions. My peephole is near the left edge of my door but the people who come through the back door of my building, who come down the hallway towards my apartment from the back of the building, these people will reach the right edge of my door, the right edge, that is, from my perspective, standing behind the door, facing out. If a person is hesitant, uncertain, he will slow as he reaches my door, he will stand to the right side of my door, unless he passes my door and then reconsiders, comes part way back, stands to the left side of the door, but if he reconsiders after passing my door, who's to say he won't pass my door again, walk fully past and wait, just to the right of the door, hand upraised, hovering? It doesn't matter. I can't see clearly through my peephole. I see greasy shapes. Looking through the peephole, I know if shapes are people, because the peephole is people height, at the midway height of middle-sized people. I see the shapes of people passing, but even then I'm often wrong. There are no people. It's the grease on the peephole. When you stare at the grease for too long it makes shapes. My peephole doesn't show people and that is what peepholes are meant to show. If squirrels came through the back door of my building, squirrels from the alley, or cats, if they ran through the hallways I wouldn't see them through my peephole, even if my peephole were clean, even if it were a convex lens magnifying to a power of ten. I would have no idea anything was happening. Crows might be flying through the building. Crows would fly above the peephole. I wouldn't see them. I would miss it. It must be wonderful, the crows in the hallway, crows turning a right angle at the end of the hallway, turning ninety degrees in the air to fly down the next hallway. I want to see the crows flying. They fly past my door. They turn. They make a right angle. Every now and then I can't stand it. I throw my door open and look out at the hallway. Nothing is happening but something has happened, must have happened, just happened. When I shut the door it starts again. I am practicing. I can open the door so much faster than when I started and

at more irregular intervals. I am becoming less pre-
dictable. I am getting closer and closer. One day soon
I will surprise it, what's happening. It can't hide from
me forever.

SUPERDOME

When I wake up, I walk around my house. It is a wreck.
"What a wreck!" I say, because I know it is a wreck, and
there is nothing deficient in my knowing. I will defend
myself against deficiencies of knowing by acceding to
the wreck, to the high office the wreck has bestowed
on my house. I am humbled in the wreck—in its lofti-
ness. I don't love it—can we love a thing we can't com-
pass?—it exceeds me. It is wrong to speak of love. It's not
love. I'm moving clockwise. It's that side of the world.
I drink my coffee and dial the phone. "Mother," I say,
"Should I buy a buffet or a hutch?" "Yes, a hut," says
my mother. "Live in a hut by the house, let the wreck
clean itself, it's a self-cleaning wreck." "Mother," I say,
"Don't you mean it's a self-cleaning house?" "Put your
head in the self-cleaning stove," says my mother. "It's
not love, but it echoes."

TRANSITION TOWN

In the morning, I left the house and found the farmer without the torch, standing beside the path. He faced away from his house, faced the path. I asked him if he had seen any strangers coming or going. I waited. I asked about animals. I waited. "Birds," the farmer said. I asked him what kinds of birds and waited, and then I asked him if any of the blood splashed on his house was new blood. "New blood," the farmer said. The resources I had given him last night covered also a meal of squashes and I went inside to find the meal prepared.

I ate at the kitchen table with the farmer's daughter. I asked her to describe the squashes and waited. "They are white, red, orange, blue, and striped," she said. I asked her what I had dreamed and waited. "You know you were underground," she said. I asked her how I had got there. I asked too quickly and waited too long. She walked out the back door with a basket half-filled with minerals. I followed her and asked if she had a message. She followed me back into the kitchen. She scratched a fork across a piece of parchment that had baked in the oven. When she folded the parchment, it broke in half. She handed me the halves and I added them to my resources.

I went and stood by the farmer on the path. The farmer faced the path and I faced the house. The splash of blood was brighter in the daylight than it had appeared by torchlight but the shape was the same. The morning advanced. I went around the farmhouse into the farmer's field and knelt down at the black verge of the unplanted quadrant. I pressed with my fingertips and the material flexed like chitin but it was hot to the touch, as though a fire burned beneath it. It was too hard to puncture with bit or blade, except in one place I knew of, where a swiveled knife yielded a hole big enough to permit my body through in pieces.

TRANSITION TOWN

I killed the statue, I lost its crystal eyes. I recruited
the living gore and took them to the pentacle, but
two armies massed and fought to my death. "It's
black throughout," said Ivor. "Let's stay in the
rooms upstairs." He and Kappa had risen and stag-
gered into benches, but Spile, rising, kept his feet.
He held still, all but his head, which he shook, as
though to say:

Insects seek liquids between the lids, lips, around
each rim; I seal these tightly, and this open wound—
too filled with teeth. Nothing enters; they circle, lay
their eggs in air. Packed with salt, this face could hold
its shape for days. Packed with snakes, launched into
the pit, this face could strike and strike. Green-rayed,
the horses stagger up. Scream and bite their flanks.
They swell and split and leak. A seizing boy rolls out
the fire. I feel my way through darkness by the points
of many tongues.

Ivor and Kappa shouted, toppled tables, boots slid-ing in broth and ale and slow to stiffen wax, arms like millwheels. I left Spile to manage. When I turned, I could see him in the mirror getting limbs in order, patting them down until they each seemed like a body all of a piece.

I did not walk for long, perhaps fifty cubits. I needed resources. Dorn sold me resources. Then I asked him questions about the path, what strangers he had seen coming or going, what manner of conversation they'd made. "Strangers," Dorn said. "Conversation." Dorn owned a wooden shop with one doorway and, inside, he stowed his resources in bins. We stood in the door-way. I faced the shop and Dorn faced the path. Dorn is not a farmer but he looks like the farmers, wears the same clothes, makes the same gestures, speaks as slowly, so I waited. "The strangers I've seen are you," Dorn said. "Today and before. You always speak about yourselves." It was hardly the kind of night to set out into, so I stood in the doorway and so did Dorn, the two of us gazing steadily over one another's shoulders.

Soon I realized I was too encumbered by resources to find standing restful and so I set out. I don't ride or track or hunt with ranged weapons. I have a small stock of memories about a time when old people were young and performed such labors as we cannot believe. Those aren't my memories. They're stories then. They can be traded.

The night was black throughout, with no limpidity in adjacent air; the darkness around my head and shoulders shone as densely as the rest. The town had sounds—creaking of wooden structures; lesser creaking of farmers' boots; creaking, lesser still, of farmers' bones, the foot bones of those farmers who paced bootless; other objects being shifted or shifting of their own accord; female voices—and I walked with the sounds on either side of me. When the sounds the town had were behind me and the sounds on either side became the sounds of fields—coughing geese; mild, de-centralized soughing of grasses; fog and droplets shifting states, one to the other and back again—I knew I was no longer walking on the path in town but walking on the path as it cut through fields.

I hoped to encounter a stranger as I walked. By stranger, I meant someone who was not like Dorn, or the other shop owners or farmers, or like Spile, Ivor, or Kappa, someone I would recognize. Once, when walking on the path, I encountered a stranger who told me a story before I greeted her or offered her payment. We approached each other, I from one of the path's directions, she from the other, and we stopped, facing one another, and she spoke.

The stranger told me about a place similar to the fields beyond the farmers' fields, the fields of boulders, but instead of boulders in the fields, there were shards. These shards were remnants of the greatest city ever built: a city of towers, a city of such height and such breadth that it couldn't be conceived of in its entirety. Even before its destruction into shards, the city did not cohere but manifested at innumerable discrete points, each point divided by vast distances in which all other points, from the vista afforded by any one, could not be seen. Every inhabitant lived unknown to all the others.

The destruction killed every inhabitant in the same way, although each death was experienced singly. The city's towers became shards scattered on the fields. The city's inhabitants became fluid and slid into the crater created by the force of the city's destruction. Flames hardened the fluid and the fluid formed a black membrane over whatever is now existent or inexistent in the depths of the crater.

The wind came up as I walked and my hair responded. My heavy cloak did not respond. Before I reached the fields of boulders, I encountered the farmer who lives in the house at the far edge of the farmers' fields. This farmer holds a torch so he is visible even in black night and he inspects the front of his house where it has been splashed with blood. I asked the farmer what he smelled and waited. "Smoke," said the farmer. "Tar. Yarn. Soil." This farmer was like Dorn, but I called him Oger. "Bowel," said Oger. "Salt. Nickel." In exchange for a portion of resources, he showed me to a cold room. I unrolled my sleeping mat.

No events.

PERFECT COMPETITION

Now the world has more riches, more water and diamonds, and there are wives enough for everyone, even the wives can have wives now, and foods grow simultaneously, hot foods and cold foods, and the grooming of the body is less painful, and the body is more productive, and the pets are prouder of their bodies, and the friends are everywhere but never take up room, and there is lots of room for everything even though everything is always getting bigger, there's always more room to be filled with foods and friends and pursuing hot and cold deportment in a range of foods and bodies and preferential for everything, inclusive wives and pets and room to keep intact their genitals and wombs and more pets and self-confidence and food, and it can't get full, there's more of it, there's information, there's cold pasta, there's the sky with the option of food inside and friends to take there with the option to put it all inside their bodies and the option to stay at home.

MEME

I bought my mother a small hospital with a decent operating budget and she picked out a rheumatologist, an oncologist, a cardiovascular surgeon, an orthopedist, and an anesthesiologist, and that used up the salary lines, but then she replaced the anesthesiologist with a nurse anesthetist and there was enough left over to add a phlebotomist and a Reiki practitioner. Architecturally, it was a very nice hospital, more like a mad house, with ivy on the walls, and expansive grounds and willow trees, and my mother, when she saw the willow trees, said, "Maybe I'll learn how to make aspirin," and I said, "Mother, I didn't buy you a hospital so you can learn how to make aspirin," and she said, "No, dear, of course not," and she said, "Does the lab here have a tablet press?" and I said, "Mother, it's a fully equipped lab," sharply, because I hadn't thought to inventory the lab and could that possible oversight point to additional oversights? And if so, what could they be? We walked inside the hospital, and I showed my mother her room. I'd arranged it so that it was nearly identical to her room in her former home. Instead of apple trees, she could see willow trees from her window and that wasn't a bad trade, an even trade I'd say. Also, there was a skylight at the end of her hall. Her former home had no such skylight. Beneath the skylight, I'd arranged a dozen massively potted aspidistras. I walked my mother to the end of the hall and she said, "This is lovely," and I said, "Thank you, Mother," and she admired the aspidistras ("These are lovely aspidistras.") and she said, "When your Uncle Billy came back..." and I said, "Poor Uncle Billy," and she said, "...he told me he felt very comfortable in Vietnam because the jungle was filled with houseplants," and I said, "Do you want an exercise bike?" and she said, "No, dear, the hallways are so long." We walked a lap around the whole first floor to get back to her room and then I said goodbye. Driving away, I felt wonderful about buying my mother the hospital. And since that first day, I've learned more about the hospital—that Al Jolson died there, and that Georgios Papanikolaou once came to give a talk—and I feel more confident than ever that I did not make a mistake, even though I failed to inventory the lab and, it turns out, check the elevator inspection notices and the generators. The lab is fine; the elevators are fine; the generators are good as new and never been used.

My mother says everything is perfectly pleasant and I feel good about that. As tens, hundreds, thousands of adult children start buying hospitals for their mothers, I feel good that, by acting quickly, I managed to buy my own mother the most desirable hospital. It's in the best area for our purposes, a rural county neither too close nor too far. I used to get phone calls about it from would-be buyers, but for months now I've kept my phone turned off, and when the contract expires I will cancel the plan altogether.

CREUTZFELDT–JAKOB

We live in the land of bad waters. When the season comes for hunting, we hunt. We string up the kills in the dooryard. We clean the kills, break them down into parts, bag the parts, and freeze them. There's no game native to this land. We hunt our own dogs, the cunning ones who slipped their chains and went wild, and the stricken ones we allowed to slink away through reeds. All of them who survive beyond our fences turn sick and vicious. They find no nourishment. They crop grass and vomit and lose their teeth. Sometimes in the yellow fog of morning, crawling up from the slough on our bellies, guns tilted so the barrels can't fill with mud or with rain, we surprise dozens of them grazing in the clearing and we pick off the choicest. We shoot also those too weak or mad to run, those who turn in circles or lap blood as though they can't see or hear or smell us moving towards them. When the rainy season comes, it's so hot the kills don't cool and the meat turns before we get the skins off. If we shoo away the flies, they struggle to rise into the air. Most roll and drop and produce foam from where they must have mouths. Then the season comes in which hunting is prohibited. We crop grass. We sit in a circle on the lowest stretch of land within our fences. White moisture rises through the grass. It dries gray on our skin. We pick at flecks. We speak or listen. The eldest among us say they remember hunting deer and eating thick stews that settled easily inside of them, but they misremember. It was dogs then too. It's always been dogs. There was nothing here before the first of us came and it was only dogs we brought with us. We don't contradict the eldest. We let them tell their stories. We like stories. We are kind to the eldest. When they speak, we listen, and when we speak, we say, yes, there must be deer somewhere.

TRANSITION TOWN

It was night. Wooden structures creaked. Boots. Bones. Dorn stood in the dark. Through the doorway, I could see that the tables had been righted. I could pay for a bath, a bed, a bowl of soup. I entered, paid and went into the rooms upstairs. I failed to distinguish Ivor from Spile. Kappa I could tell by the crystal eyes balanced in the sockets. I took them. Downstairs, I mingled. I ate a bowl of soup. My constitution improved. A farmer ate beef. I asked the farmer, what news. The farmer stood. "Gourd," said the farmer. "Sorghum." I stood, opened the map, held it by his face. "Beef," said the farmer. "Mullet." I thought. I said, "Tower." I waited. I said, "Flame." I waited. The farmer waited. He is not a stranger, one like me, who desires only to be someplace else. He is the farmer who is here, eating beef. He has a beard and boots, a small knife for cutting meat, knows of gourds.

I looked at the map. There is the town, dark dot, there are the farmers' fields. The fields are long green swaths, interspersed with brown: quadrants of cleared forest, yet unplanted. Beyond the farmers' fields, fields of boulders, then low hills begin, undulant lines, plateau in yellow, more green, black slashes and shards, then tree symbols labeled "Hacktern Woods:" wet spruce, a river, rapids, surface and underwater rocks marked with Xs, Lake Mosst, higher hills in paler green, grasslands, X'ed encampments of mercenary tribes, umber desert, inland sea, ring of cliffs, mountains, violet, very high, black downs, black bog, the white region where the paper curls back. The map is not to scale.

Featureless dark stretches across a portion of corresponding hexes, always shifting. I have put pinholes in the map and peered through, but nothing shines to indicate shaft or chamber, vein of glowing ore, shadow flame of the abyss. Standing on the path, the map held out, I have seen on occasion the half-devoured sun, its decrescent fire projected on the dust. In the region underneath our feet the death that streams towards us from above has already come. This is the journey I will repeat while I can, into the depths and up again. I don't learn from it, but I pass the time. I will keep moving between, until there is only one world, a single point, all things fused, continuous, without light.

ACKNOWLEDGMENTS

I am grateful to the editors of the following magazines and journals, in which versions of several stories from *The Week* first appeared: *NOON, Pushcart Prize XXVIII, Conjunctions, Black Warrior Review, 3 A.M. Magazine, Verse, Post Road, Tupelo Quarterly, Delirious Hem, Locomotive, Loose Change, Threadcount, elsewhere, No Tell Motel,* and *LIT magazine.*

Thanks to Brian Kiteley for all the generosities and guidance. Thanks also to Christine Gardiner, Robert Urquhart, Marream Krollos, Laird Hunt, and Bin Ramke, for reading and for support.

Thanks to Broc Rossell, a forever comrade, for the vision and the work it takes.